BIRDIE
IN BRUGES

HEIDI WILLIAMSON

Originally published as *Legend of the Lost Aventurine* under the pen name Heidi English.

Copyediting by The Blue Garret
Book Cover Design by ebooklaunch.com
Published by Flyaway Ink Creative

For the daydreamers

A village
  grieves for its soul
its families
  vanished
its houses
  empty
its shops
  deserted
its life
  extinguished
so only ghosts remain.

PROLOGUE

Bruges, Belgium
April 1499

"What do you know of the witch's daughter?"

"The witch's... daughter?" Henri's thin legs quaked as his toes strained to touch the ground.

"*Oui*, you fool."

There'd been rumors at school of a swirling sorceress who conjured potions from the icy waters of the North Sea. Maybe she was the witch's daughter.

But that couldn't be it.

No. Certainly not. Henri's father, who was well versed in such things, had dismissed the rumors as rubbish when he'd dared to mention them one winter evening as they warmed themselves by the fire in the parlor.

"Henri, my son." He'd leaned in close, tapping sweet-smelling tobacco into his pipe. "I sail the dreaded North Sea each time I leave you. A fortnight ago I crossed it as I returned from the mighty Rhine River, where rumors flow not of a sorceress, but of a lovely blond maiden called the Loreley who lures sailors to their deaths upon the jagged rocks."

He puffed into the end of his carved pipe as he swirled a flame across its ivory bowl, briefly illuminating his bearded face. Only then did he continue, his light eyes twinkling as he met his son's gaze. "I can assure you there is not a woman in all of Belgium – sorceress or no – powerful enough to tame those wicked waters."

Clearly his father had not met this girl – this wicked girl – who now held him so firmly he feared he'd never escape. Henri had a dim recollection of seeing the girl before, but he couldn't place where. Her face had been pretty then, not strained with anger and hunger as it was now.

A gaggle of boys milled nearby on the canal bank, watching the proceedings with muted curiosity.

Henri struggled to breathe as the girl tightened her grip. He wished he'd never wandered back here beyond the red brick brewery on the edge of town.

He kicked, but met only air.

The sky snapped with the energy of a coming storm. In the distance, canal boats were moored near the busy *Markt*, weighed down with goods from far-off lands. Bulky shapes moved in the fading light as the seafaring crews hastened to secure a hard drink and a soft place to sleep before the skies opened.

Somewhere close by a bird wailed, its normal song

distorted and panicked. Henri's gaze darted to locate the source of the sound.

He spotted a dove several yards away and his heart sank. The pitiful creature had been snared. Several of the boys surrounded it, ready to play a game he'd heard of but never witnessed firsthand.

The girl gave Henri another rough shake and then dropped him at her feet. His legs crumpled beneath him at the surprise release.

He met her dull blue eyes, the dove forgotten.

"The witch's daughter haunts all who tread here," she warned. "She'll chase you in your dreams until you wake screaming and even your *maman* cannot save you."

Two of the boys broke away from the dove and made their way toward Henri. One was tall, with a rat-like face and a crushed hat. The other was shorter, with blond hair that hung in ringlets across a long forehead.

"Her eyes are dead sockets and she smells of mice and demons," the taller of the two sneered as he circled him.

"She casts spells that make your skin shrivel and slide from your bones," the other added, falling in step behind the first.

A low voice cut through the taunts. "What should I do with him?"

It was a boy who was bigger than the others, and older than the girl. Henri hadn't noticed him before. He lounged against the canal wall as if bored with the latest turn in their day.

"Bury him like a bird." A lanky boy standing not far from the dove picked up a heavy stone from the ground. He tossed it into the air to feel its weight.

Henri scrambled backward to his feet and, remembering his station for the first time since wandering into this nest of ne'er-do-wells, puffed his chest and raised his chin.

He was younger than the children who surrounded him, but he was a LeFort and, even here, he knew that meant something.

The girl leaned in, her breath hot on his face.

"Cours," she whispered. "Run."

Henri blinked. He didn't know what he expected, but it wasn't that.

He took a half step back, then bolted up the dirt path toward the Minnewater park, whose iron gates would release him to the freedom of the busy cobblestone lanes beyond.

In the Middle Ages, Bruges was the richest city in Belgium. Its thriving port welcomed merchants from across the known world, and its markets rivaled only those of Venice. But by the 1500s, the town was all but abandoned. It remained that way, a mysterious time capsule near the sea, until tourists rediscovered its charms in the Romantic age.

—*Marty McEntire*, Europe for Americans Travel Guide

CHAPTER ONE

Bruges, Belgium
Present day

Birdie Blessing, a fifteen-year-old American with an
unfortunate name and cheap luggage, tailed her mom
through slippery cobblestone lanes at twilight on the longest
day of the year. They'd missed their connecting train to
Bruges at the sprawling station in Brussels, and now they
were running late.

"Keep up. It's just a few more blocks."

Birdie tugged on the hand-me-down suitcase, its scratchy
wheels skittering across the uneven stones. The purple case
tilted hard to the right, twisting her wrist. As she struggled to
tame it, her backpack straps slid down her shoulders, gluing
her arms to her sides. She dropped the suitcase and
glowered at it.

High above, a church bell tolled, just once, then quieted
as the deep note faded in the distance. She tilted her head to

the sky. The blue-black night pressed the pinks and oranges of a stormy sunset toward the west.

Toward home.

"Come on, let's go," her mom called without turning around, raising her voice above the clamor of her own luggage on the cobblestones. "Or we'll get locked out of the bed-and-breakfast."

Birdie hoisted her backpack onto her shoulders once more and cinched the straps down hard. As she bent to reclaim the suitcase, she locked eyes with a lanky boy loitering on a stoop several doors down. She teetered back, drawing the suitcase close.

He flashed a crooked smile, then took a step forward. As he did, an image of her brother, teasing and laughing at her, swept into her mind.

She wrinkled her nose and willed it away. She couldn't think about Jonah right now. Even if everything was his fault.

Not hers.

His.

No matter what everyone said.

"Birdie?" Her mom stood staring down the narrow lane at her, hands on her hips.

The boy sank back onto the stoop and disappeared into the shadows.

"Coming!" She hurried on long legs to catch up to her mom, who'd started walking again and was already several yards ahead. The church bell tolled as she fell in step behind her.

Birdie glanced up from her footing long enough to spot

the old gray bell tower rising off-kilter above the pointed roofs of the town's Gothic buildings. They leaned heavily against one another in the deepening light, each dependent on the next for support after centuries of standing together.

The bell tolled again. Was that twice? Or had she missed one? She checked her watch. 9:49 p.m. Why was the stupid thing ringing at all?

She peeked over her shoulder to make sure the boy hadn't followed her, and her sneaker caught the edge of a jagged cobblestone. She tumbled forward, barely catching herself with her free hand before she crashed onto the lane. She squeezed her eyes closed.

"I'm in no danger here," she whispered.

"What did you say, Birdie?"

"Nothing." She scrambled to her feet as she opened her eyes and flicked a piece of gravel from the heel of her palm. She tugged on the tie that held her long chestnut hair until it fell in a comforting wave against her back, hiding her pale face from unwelcome eyes.

The bell had struck its last note by the time they reached a small square where a half-dozen curving lanes and alleys converged. Her mom dug around in her purse for the map. It was the last thing she'd printed before tucking the printer and the computer into moving boxes.

"Are we lost?"

"No." She pivoted slowly as she compared the names on the map with the hand-painted street signs bolted just above the first story of each corner building. She flipped the map upside down and held it high to capture the last of the light. "But this town is a maze."

Birdie leaned into her suitcase.

Her dad had been an awesome navigator. They never got lost.

Until now.

Now they were people who got lost. People who missed trains. People who didn't have a clue what they were doing.

"Ah, there we go. This way." Her mom pointed to a stone archway on the far side of the square.

"Are you sure?"

A rumble sounded behind them, fast and low.

Birdie dropped the suitcase and grabbed her mom's arm, pulling her back against the weathered wooden door of a chocolate shop as a pair of headlights swept over them. A black sedan flew by, so close that her hair lifted from her shoulders in its wake.

"What the..." Birdie began as her mom shook loose from her grip.

"Maniac!" Mrs. Blessing charged out into the middle of the lane. "You... maniac!"

A few people smoking outside a nearby tavern snickered.

"Let's just go." Birdie retrieved her suitcase. "It's that way, right? Come on, Mom."

Accommodations in Bruges range from high-end,
full-service hotels to cheery youth hostels. In between are
bed-and-breakfasts, which many of my readers find offer the
best value for the price. Reserve early and mention this book to
receive my special Marty McEntire rate.

—*Marty McEntire,* Europe for Americans Travel Guide

CHAPTER TWO

The next morning dawned brightly as sunlight filtered through the open window of their attic bedroom and settled on Birdie's eyelids. In her dream, the opening notes of a familiar song repeated, tugging her awake.

It was way too early for music.

"Turn it down, people." Her voice was scratchy, and her body felt like lead on the soft mattress.

She opened one eye, squinting against the light. The notes came again, echoing against the medieval houses that hugged the lane below, which was so narrow she'd wondered last night if she could touch both sides if she spread her arms wide.

They'd made it to the bed-and-breakfast with a few minutes to spare, even after missing the swinging sign with the bear on it that hung out front, forcing them to backtrack. Her mom had punched a code into a glowing green keypad that looked out of place against the old masonry, and then they'd quietly climbed the three flights of stairs to their cozy room.

WOO who…

There it was again. Seriously? Were there workers outside? Didn't they have rules about this kind of thing?

She perched on her elbows and peered outside. She thought about climbing out of bed to get a better view, but the breeze was cool on her bare arms, and the yellow duvet's warmth seemed far more inviting than the wooden floor.

A ray of sunlight danced along the rafters to the foot of the twin bed where her mom was sleeping, her breath slow and gentle, her new blond highlights fanned out around her face. Birdie sent a thank you to the stars. It'd been ages since she'd seen her rest so peacefully.

She turned back to the open window as a gray-and-white dove glided to the sill. Its wobbly gaze darted to the cobblestone lane three stories below, then up to the bright blue sky. From far away, the crisp notes of the song sounded again, carried across the morning air.

WOO WHO!

Birdie buried her head beneath the duvet as the dove's answer ricocheted across the room.

"What on earth?" her mom grumbled, her voice barely audible. "That sounds like the beginning of a song."

Birdie peeked over the edge of the duvet as she twisted in the soft bed to look at her mom. "That's exactly what I thought. I dreamed somebody kept playing it. Then Willy showed up."

"Who's Willy?"

"The dove."

"You named him?" She looked as if she might laugh, but

held back. "Why? And why Willy?"

Birdie shrugged. "Willy or won't he wake us up every morning?"

Her mom settled deeper into the mattress. "Glad to see you're getting your sense of humor back."

Birdie swallowed, the words washing over her like ice water. She punched her pillow to fluff it, then rolled back toward the window to try to forget she'd heard them.

"Well, I guess I'm awake now," her mom said with a sigh. "But it's early. According to the guidebook, breakfast starts at eight. I'm grabbing a shower." The bed squeaked as she stood. "And Birdie?"

She continued to stare out the open window. "Hmmm?"

"Do not let Willy fly in here."

She hadn't considered that possibility.

Fortunately, Willy had little interest in exploring the attic of the bed-and-breakfast. He called to the other dove for a while, then latched his beady eyes on Birdie's hazel ones, dipped low as if he were bowing, and flew off in a rustle of wings and air.

At his departure, she threw back the duvet and stepped to the window on bare feet. A handful of feathers that resembled small quill pens lay scattered on the broad stone windowsill. She glanced over her shoulder to make sure the bathroom door was still closed, then reached out to retrieve them. As she did, the sun sparkled off an object a few inches away.

She bent forward to get a better look and clunked her head against the glass. She rubbed the pain away as she cranked the window open as far as it would go. When she was sure her shoulders would fit, she leaned through the slender opening.

The sun flashed against the object again, making its surface sparkle as if it were on fire.

Birdie stretched through the window as far as she could, but she still couldn't reach it, even with her fingertips. She checked the bathroom door again, then lifted off the floor, teetering across the windowsill until she could just touch it.

She felt for the shiny stone, cool and smooth beneath her fingers. She raked it toward the window, but as she did, it caught on a rough part of the sill and flipped farther away.

She stopped, transfixed by its brilliant sheen as it rocked halfway off the ledge.

She had to have it now. She leaned a precarious inch further out the window, flexing her toes against the wall. An inch more, and she grasped it.

Behind her, the latch of the bathroom door slid open.

Birdie wriggled back into the room, cranked the window to its previous position, then spun to face her mother.

"Ready for breakfast?" Mrs. Blessing emerged, dressed in casual clothes and looking refreshed. She draped her nightgown over a rickety desk chair. "It's in the dining room."

Across town, a bell began its sluggish chime.

"I'll get ready." Birdie dove for her suitcase, retrieved a T-shirt and a pair of jeans, and pushed the stone deep into the front pocket. She gathered the rest of her clothes for the day and headed for the bathroom.

"Make sure you wash your hands if you were handling

those feathers."

Birdie had forgotten about the feathers. "Right," she said.

Breakfasts in Europe vary from country to country.
The further north you travel, the heartier the fare.
The further south? Get used to croissants and jam.

—*Marty McEntire,* Europe for Americans Travel Guide

CHAPTER THREE

Twenty minutes later, Birdie followed her mom down the stairs into a beautiful foyer, through a sunny sitting room, and into the dining room, where a handful of guests were already seated around a single long table.

"No, Harry, I don't think that's right," a jolly-looking woman was saying. She sat at the far end of the table, examining a multicolored map through a thin pair of reading glasses. The elegant drapes behind her were thrown open, revealing a crumbling brick wall crawling with ivy.

"Oh, for Pete's sake. Let me see that map." Harry's bushy white mustache wiggled as he spoke.

The woman handed it to him, shaking her head as she did. "I can't find Widger or Winger or What Ever Street it is anywhere."

"It's right here, Helga." He smoothed the map on the fabric tablecloth and pointed to a spot on it. "Wijngaardstraat. You don't need to add street at the end: *straat* means street."

Birdie glanced at her mom and saw the corner of her

mouth twitch.

"Oh. Well, how am I supposed to know that?"

"Marty explained it in the book."

Helga squared her ample shoulders and looked as if she were about to object, but Harry spoke first.

"It doesn't matter." He tapped the map with a thick index finger. "We'll take that when we get close to the old Begijnhof where the nuns lived. It can't be more than a fifteen-minute walk from here."

"Well, look at that." She peered through her glasses to the spot where Harry was tapping. "It's right there."

She glanced up from the map and winked at a tall boy sitting across from her. She removed her glasses, folded them carefully, and set them beside her plate. "Maybe it's time for a fresh pair."

The boy managed a smile that looked crooked on his angular face.

Crooked and oddly familiar.

Before Birdie could study him further, a sturdy woman bustled through a swinging door at the far side of the room. She wore her silver-and-gold hair twisted high in a bun, and carried a steaming plate of bacon.

Mrs. Blessing nudged Birdie toward the table.

"Ah, good morning," the woman said in a crisp Dutch accent, noticing the newcomers at once. Her face lit with a welcoming smile. She gestured to two empty chairs with the plate of bacon. "Come, sit, sit. You must be the Blessings. Welcome to t'Bruges Huis. I'm Mrs. Devon. Would you like coffee? Juice?"

"Coffee would be wonderful," Mrs. Blessing said. "Thank

you."

"And you?" she asked as she scooped several slices of bacon onto the boy's plate. "Orange juice, I think?"

"Yes, thank you," Birdie said.

"Very good." She bumped her hip against the door and it swung open wide, revealing a cheery kitchen beyond.

"Good morning," Helga said as she shifted forward to get a better look at them. "I'm Helga and this is my husband, Harry. We're from Ohio. Akron."

"Nice to meet you. I'm Maria and this is my daughter, Birdie. We're from Pennsylvania."

"Whereabouts?" Harry asked.

"Bamburg?"

"Oh, sure. I've heard of Bamburg." His voice had a booming quality that filled the room. "There's a college there."

"Yes, that's right."

"And what brings you to the fine city of Bruges?"

Birdie's heart quickened, but her mom didn't miss a beat.

"I'm a designer," she said. "We're exploring Europe this summer to get ideas for a new line of clothing and home accessories I'm working on. It has a medieval theme."

"Just the two of you?" Helga asked, leaning on her generous elbows. "What a wonderful excuse to see the Old World."

Birdie stole a glance at the boy sitting next to her as the women talked. He was much taller than she was, and much taller than Jonah had been, but she thought he was about her age.

He caught her looking at him and grinned awkwardly

through a mouthful of bacon.

Birdie's gaze darted to her empty plate, her cheeks growing warm.

Mrs. Devon bustled back into the dining room with the drinks.

"Have you met Ben?" She set a bright glass of fresh-squeezed juice on Birdie's placemat. "He's visiting Bruges with his uncle. Will Mr. Martin be joining us this morning?"

Ben finished chewing and swallowed another large bite. "Afraid not. He's still upstairs, ma'am."

His tone was deeper than Birdie expected, and rich with a subtle drawl. Definitely American.

"He was fixing to get some work done, so I came down without him."

"Yes, the young men are always hungry," Mrs. Devon said. "I've seen many like you at this table, and always they are hungry, yes?"

A memory of Jonah sitting on the patio devouring ears of corn on the cob slipped across Birdie's consciousness. She pushed it away. She thought she saw a shadow cross her mom's face too.

"Yes, ma'am."

"How long have you been running the bed-and-breakfast?" Helga asked.

"Thirty years."

"It's just lovely. So elegant."

"Yes. It was my mother's house." She looked at Birdie. "And breakfast for you?"

She picked an omelet, toast, and bacon and Mrs. Devon slipped into the kitchen to prepare it.

"We found this place in the *Europe for Americans Travel Guide*," Helga said after the door closed. "Have you heard of it? It's the best guidebook I've ever read. The author, Marty McEntire, is full of great tips and he is so funny too." She yanked the book from a large bag hanging on the back of her chair.

Birdie recognized the green and yellow cover at once.

Her mom chuckled. "Marty helped me plan this entire trip. That book's been like my bible."

"Yeah, my uncle has that book," Ben said. "He has another one too. It's a guide to every brewery and bar in eleven countries."

Birdie raised her eyebrows at him.

He raised his back at her. They were dark and a little bushy, setting off the deep brown eyes beneath them. His hair was brownish black and reminded Birdie of an untamed mop.

And of their walk from the train station the night before.

"Yes, we met your Uncle Noah yesterday. He's a brew-master. You're from Texas. Austin, right?"

Ben broke his stare with Birdie.

"Not exactly, ma'am. I'm from Marshall Falls, but Uncle Noah's from Austin. He's not a brew-master yet, but he sure wants to be."

"Oh yes, that's right, that's right. Our granddaughter is here too." She eyed the sitting room.

Birdie followed her gaze, but there was no one there.

"Not up yet," Harry grumbled.

"No, I suppose not." Helga paused, sizing up Birdie and Ben with friendly blue eyes. "You can meet her later. Her name is Kayla. She's about your age, I think. Seventeen."

"Oh, I'm fifteen," Birdie said.

"Fifteen," Ben said with a nod.

"Well, she's older then." Helga didn't bother to hide a sigh.

The kitchen door swung open, and Mrs. Devon returned with the Blessings' breakfasts. She set the plates on the mats. "And what about you, young man? Anything else from the kitchen?"

"No thank you, ma'am, I'm good." He reached for a raspberry pastry on the top tier of a serving stand in the center of the table laden with goodies. "This should do it."

"Well, are you about ready?" Harry pushed his chair back. He seemed entirely too big for the small piece of furniture.

Helga wiped her mouth with the cloth napkin that had been covering her lap. "I am. Should we wake Kayla for breakfast?"

Harry frowned, and the edges of his white mustache descended like curtains around his lips. "We should have woken her up two hours ago."

"Well, too late now. No use getting upset about it." Helga turned to the Blessings. "It was so nice to meet you both. Enjoy your time exploring Bruges today. You're going to love it. We've been here three days and we could stay a dozen more."

"Thank you. You too," Mrs. Blessing said.

Birdie dug into the omelet, trying to remember the last time she'd had a hot breakfast. At home, she grabbed cereal or yogurt from an almost empty fridge, if she bothered to eat at all.

"What are we doing today?" she asked as she finished her toast.

Her mom was staring at the sunshine pooling on the sitting room floor. She glanced at Birdie as if she'd forgotten she was there. "Well, I thought we'd rent bikes and explore the town that way. There's a rental shop a couple of blocks away. When you're done with breakfast, we can get ready and go."

"Done." Birdie wiped her hands and tossed the napkin on the table.

"Okay, great. I'll run to the room to get my things and then we can leave. Do you need anything?"

"Nope, I'm good. I already have my daypack. I'll just wait in the foyer." She stood to leave.

"Okay." Mrs. Blessing leaned around Birdie. "Bye, Ben."

He nodded farewell as he reached for another pastry.

"Bye, Birdie," he said with a grin.

The Basilica of the Holy Blood houses Bruges's most famous relic, a flask said to contain a drop of the blood of Jesus. The Count of Flanders sent it to Bruges in the thirteenth century, along with other items looted from Constantinople during the Crusades. You'll find relics – drops of blood, fragments of bone, sometimes entire skeletons – sprinkled at churches all across Europe. The most influential churches received the most coveted relics.

—*Marty McEntire*, Europe for Americans Travel Guide

CHAPTER FOUR

After breakfast, Birdie settled on the second-to-last step in the mirrored foyer, her chin tucked into her hands as she leaned forward, elbows on her knees. The patchwork daypack holding her sketchbook, pencils, camera, and jacket sat beside her. She wished she had her phone, but her mother hadn't let her bring it.

"Who are you planning to call?" her mom had asked.

"No one. But I'd like to take pictures."

"Bring a camera."

That had been the end of the conversation and she hadn't seen her phone since. She assumed it was packed with everything else in the storage unit at home. She could have fought to bring it – and her mom might have given in – but there was no one to call, no one to text, no one to communicate with at all. And Lord knew no one would send her a message.

She tried to forget about her phone and the mess she now called her life. If there was one good thing about spending the summer in Europe with her mom, it was that she could escape for a while. No one knew her here. No one knew the story. She could be anyone.

Maybe even someone normal.

She stared absently at the mosaic tiles that coalesced into a flower on the floor. A few of the pieces had chipped over time or were missing altogether. But she could tell that someone had positioned each tiny tile to create a flowing pattern of colorful ribbons. A single deep-red ribbon punctuated them all. She tracked it to the center of the bloom, where it exploded into different shades.

As she followed the sweep of a brown ribbon of tiles, she remembered the sparkling stone. She half stood, dug into the pocket of her jeans to retrieve it, and then settled back down on the step.

She turned the cool piece over in her palm.

It was a lot like a river stone, about the size of a quarter, only more oblong than round. It appeared as dark as cinnamon at first, but a closer inspection revealed a golden sheen that spread like glowing sand across it.

She rubbed the surface with her thumb, enjoying the smooth feel of it against her warm skin. As she rubbed, the golden speckles shimmered and appeared to swim. It seemed to grow warmer too.

"Whatcha got there?" Ben asked as he came out of the sitting room. His angular face and crooked smile marked him as harmless despite his towering size. Now that he was standing, she could see that he wore tan cargo shorts and that his black T-shirt had a flaming guitar on it.

"I'm not sure." She opened her hand wider. "I found it

on the windowsill this morning." She turned it over on her palm to show him.

Her breath caught.

The speckles weren't just shimmering on this side; they were flowing and undulating toward the center, creating rivers of golden light.

"Whoa, that's awesome." He took a knee beside her to get a better look. As they watched, the rivers of gold collided and formed a glistening flower, just like the one on the floor at her feet. It was stunning, like a brilliant jewel set in a copper pool.

"I think it's the flower that's on the floor."

Ben lifted the toe of his skate sneaker. "You know, I think you're right."

"It's hot too." Birdie shifted it into her other hand. "Feel it."

She dropped it onto his palm.

"Holy crow, you're not kidding." He leaned in to study the golden flower. "You said you found it on the windowsill?"

Birdie nodded.

"Crazy. Where do you think it came from?"

"I have no idea."

"Maybe the last person in your room left it." He turned it over on his palm as a slow smile spread across his face. "Stinks to be them. This thing is pretty freaking cool."

"Are you looking forward to your day exploring Bruges?" Mrs. Devon said, startling them both. They'd been concentrating so hard they hadn't heard her come into the foyer.

"Oh, uh, yes I am," Birdie replied, as Ben dropped the

small stone back into her hand. She wrapped her fingers around it, shielding it from sight. Its heat radiated into her skin.

"Yeah, me too." Ben got back to his feet. "Uncle Noah and I are going to the brewery."

"You may see aventurine in the brewery gift shop." Mrs. Devon nodded toward Birdie's closed hand. "There's a legend about it – a story about the shifting sands of time. They say it was quite rare, a special glass made only in Venice."

"Aventurine?" Birdie asked.

"Yes. That's the toy in your hand. Aventurine. Like adventure, but no *d*. It looks like stone, but it's glass. Well, yours is probably plastic."

Birdie and Ben exchanged glances.

Mrs. Devon leaned against a dark cabinet, twisting a dishtowel in her hands. "True aventurine was so beautiful that everyone thought it was a gemstone, a jewel. I don't remember the whole story, but once upon a time everyone wanted one. Pilgrims spent their whole lives searching for a piece."

"Pilgrims?" Birdie asked.

"Pilgrims, yes. Well, right. You have studied United States history at school? There were pilgrims long before the ones who crossed the ocean to search for religious freedom in America. There are still pilgrims today. A pilgrim is someone who goes on a pilgrimage."

Birdie shifted the aventurine to her other hand. It was still warm, but not as hot as it had been. She watched it while Mrs. Devon continued. Even with its dark color, it was translucent, like glass. The gold speckles had floated within the opaque space as they formed the flower.

"A pilgrimage is a journey, usually a very long journey, that's important to someone's spiritual beliefs or religion. The Pilgrims went to the New World to practice their religion. Other pilgrims walk from country to country to visit cathedrals or temples as a way of showing their devotion to God. Some pilgrims come to Bruges even now to visit our Basilica of the Holy Blood."

"What about the glass?" Ben asked.

"Well, that was a symbol of earlier beliefs based on magic and mysticism. In the very early Middle Ages, before Christianity took hold, people would spend their whole lives searching for that special piece of glass."

"Why?" Birdie asked.

Mrs. Devon shrugged. "Because it was magic."

"And now they sell it at the brewery?" Ben asked as a chorus of ringing church bells drifted through the open sitting-room windows.

"Well, yes," Mrs. Devon said with a snort. "They are not the real Venetian glass. The toys go along with the legend. Souvenirs for the tourists, that's all. I don't know anyone who lives in Bruges who has one."

"Oh." Birdie ran her fingers over its smooth surface. The flower held tight. It didn't seem like a toy to her, at least not the kind she'd ever played with. "They must be expensive."

"No, not expensive at all." Mrs. Devon stood straighter and wiped her hands on the towel.

A door opened at the far end of the hall, and a stocky man in a broad hat and long coat entered.

It must be cooler outside than she thought.

The man knelt and ran a dirty hand over the tiles near the door, then pulled a small tool from his ill-fitting coat. He began prying up one of the miniature tiles.

Ben and Birdie exchanged curious glances, but Mrs. Devon didn't seem bothered by his appearance.

Upstairs, a door slammed shut, as if caught by a breeze, followed by the beat of someone hurrying down the hall.

"Are you sure you have everything you need, Birdie?" Mrs. Blessing called as she turned the corner at the top of the landing.

Birdie and Ben rose to let her mom pass by them.

"I think so." She pulled the jacket from her daypack and slipped it on, zipping the aventurine into the pocket.

"And where are you headed today?" Mrs. Devon asked.

"We're planning to rent bikes and explore the town."

"It's a beautiful day for biking. There's a chance for storms this afternoon, but otherwise, it should be cool and sunny."

"I just need to find the bike shop. Can you point me in the right direction?" Mrs. Blessing unfolded her map on the cabinet and outlined the route she thought they should take.

As the women discussed the map, Ben caught Birdie's eye and nodded toward the door at the end of the hall.

"Where did he go?" Birdie mouthed.

Ben shrugged.

"Yes, yes, that's perfect," Mrs. Devon said. "Just watch for this turn." She pointed to an intersection on the map. "It's barely an alleyway. That's where most people get lost."

Another rumble of feet sounded above them and they

took a collective step away from the bottom of the stairs.

A man in his late thirties or early forties with shaggy brown hair and dark eyes appeared on the landing. Like Ben, he wore cargo shorts and a black T-shirt.

"Morning," he said, slowing his descent when he realized there were other people there. "Ready, Ben?"

"Yes, sir."

Birdie looked from one to the other. Their resemblance was striking. They were both tall with hair that was just a bit too long to be respectable, although Ben's was a shade darker. Even their dark brown eyes caught the light similarly. If she hadn't already heard this was Ben's uncle, she would have guessed they were related.

"Ben tells me you're off to our brewery today," Mrs. Devon said in the same pleasant tone she'd used with Mrs. Blessing.

"Yes, ma'am, and we need to get a move on if we're going to make the first tour."

Ben stepped toward the front door.

"No breakfast, then?"

"Uh, no ma'am, not today. Thank you though," Uncle Noah said. "Ben, did you eat?"

He nodded.

"Okay, let's go then." Uncle Noah tipped his shaggy head at the rest of them and pulled the door open. A moment later, he and Ben were gone.

Perhaps the best way to explore Bruges is by getting lost
deep in its streets and parks on a bicycle, away from
the tour bus groups that overrun the Market Square.
Save your shopping for later in the day, when the crowds thin
and the stylish clothing and shoe stores beckon. Be sure to indulge
in the plentiful samples at the chocolate shops too. No trip to
Belgium is complete without chocolate.

—*Marty McEntire,* Europe for Americans Travel Guide

CHAPTER FIVE

"Mom?" Birdie called a few hours later as they bumped across the cobblestones on their rented bikes. She stole a glance at the dark clouds pulsing against the blue sky.

"I know, Birdie."

They turned down an alley to escape the wind and dead-ended into a crowded courtyard. Groups of people huddled under red table umbrellas and eyed the sky.

Mrs. Blessing braked as she pointed to a bike rack near the entrance to an old brick building. "There. Quickly!"

Birdie dismounted and jogged her bike around the tables as the first fat drops of rain fell. She shoved the front tire between the metal bars and grabbed her daypack from the basket. Her mom twisted the keys in the bike locks, then they sprinted up the stairs and into the building.

"Whew!" Mrs. Blessing fluffed the rain from her hair. "We made it."

"Made it where?" Birdie said as she squeezed between a white-haired man in golf shorts and a family speaking

Chinese. She brushed the raindrops from her bare arms, shivered, then pulled out her jacket and slipped it back on.

"Well," Mrs. Blessing said, sliding in beside Birdie as she glanced around the room, "we're at the brewery."

Thunder clapped and hail pelted the single-pane windows.

Her mom leaned in close to be heard over the rumble. "Want to take a tour?"

"Sure. Why not? It's better than getting soaked."

"There might be some excellent designs inside, who knows?" She rummaged in her purse for her wallet. "I'll get tickets."

"I'll check out the gift shop."

As her mom jostled through the crowd and got in line, Birdie made her way to the gift shop to scout for aventurine. She wanted to see if Mrs. Devon was right when she said they sold them here, and if she was, how much they cost.

It didn't take long to spot them. The copper-colored stones packed a bin along the far wall, close to several other bins stuffed with trinkets. One held tiny Dutch windmills, another miniature carillons.

She picked up a carillon and twirled the metal handle that jutted from its side. A hollow, mechanical song played, briefly attracting the attention of the other shoppers, who quickly lost interest when they saw her standing with the toy.

"Hey, Birdie."

She fumbled the carillon and almost dropped it.

"Whoa, sorry. Didn't mean to scare you."

"You didn't... Ben? Wait. You're still here?" She clicked the handle back into place and the music stopped. She set the toy back in its bin.

"Oh, yeah. We're still here. Don't think we'll be leaving anytime soon, either."

"Where's your uncle?"

He nodded toward the ticket line.

"You haven't done your tour yet? What have you been doing?"

"Oh, we've been on the tour. But Uncle Noah has more questions, so we're going again."

"We're going on the next one too."

"Cool. It's not so bad. It's about beer, you know? Hey, did you see the toys Mrs. Devon told us about? They're right here. There's a sign, too, with the legend on it."

"English tour!" a woman called from the front of the store. "English tour starts now!"

"Ben?" Uncle Noah towered over the other patrons as he crossed the gift shop. "Time to go."

Ben looked like he was going to ignore his uncle, but then he relented. "Later, Birdie."

"Yeah, okay. See you later."

She watched the rest of the crowd gather near the tasting room. Her mom joined them and motioned to her. Birdie took one last look at the toy bins, wishing she had time to read the legend, then maneuvered through the shop to join the others.

Belgium is world renowned for its beer, and the quirky brewery in Bruges lives up to the hype. Try to catch the first or last tour of the day to avoid the rush. Each tour ends with a free glass of their signature brew.

—*Marty McEntire*, Europe for Americans Travel Guide

CHAPTER SIX

"Usually, we begin in the courtyard," the tour guide announced. She'd herded them onto a broad covered porch. "But not today, okay?"

She gestured to the rain, which was coating the now-deserted tables and chairs. Half-full glasses of beer stood abandoned as the wind whipped the decorative umbrellas meant to protect them.

"Good idea," Uncle Noah said.

Birdie glanced at Ben, and he lifted two fingers in acknowledgment.

"*Hallo*, yes, welcome. Good afternoon." The group arranged itself in an arc around the guide, who was far shorter than any of the people on the tour. She sported a delighted smile, a pixie haircut, and close-set brown eyes that twinkled with mischief as she spoke.

"My name is Elsa. I speak English, yes? But it is not my first language so I make mistakes, okay? Already I am sorry if I make any."

"Your English sounds great to me," Ben said.

"Oh, yes, thank you very much." Her cheeks went pink. "So, yes. I am Elsa and we will spend the next, oh, hour or so together in the brewery. We will go up" – she pointed to the top of the building – "many stairs, okay? But you will see the new and the old and learn how we make the famous Belgian beer."

The brewery, Elsa told them, was first mentioned in the town's historical documents in the 1500s. Although it changed hands over time, the current brew-masters still used recipes perfected over centuries.

Elsa led them through a wide steel door into a bright, clean brewery that was at architectural odds with the wooden porch and crumbling brick outside. The air smelled of homemade bread and apple cider vinegar.

"This is the newest part of the brewery. It has the most modern equipment for making beer. We make batches here, and then send them through a wonderful underground pipeline to a factory where the beer gets bottled. The beer we make here is also in our tasting room, which – don't worry – you will visit later. It is also for sale in bottles in the gift shop."

She took a moment to explain the types of storage tanks in the room. "Any questions before we move on?"

"What is that?" Ben pointed to a foot-tall silver statue perched in an alcove near the ceiling. It was old and out of place among the stainless steel tanks.

"Oh!" Elsa grinned. "That is our dear St. Arnold, the patron saint of beer. He saved Bruges by making everyone drink."

A chuckle ran through the group.

"Yes, yes. It is true." Elsa shook her head as if she couldn't believe it herself. "St. Arnold was a monk. He came to Bruges during an outbreak of plague. Plague, as you know, was a terrible sickness that caused your skin to erupt in great oozing boils, and then, you died."

Elsa wrinkled her nose. "Yes, very fast people died. The rats contaminated the water, you see, and there were no antibiotics to treat it. Two-thirds of Europe died in this Black Death. But our St. Arnold saw that none of the men who worked at the brewery were sick. Then he realized the workers drank beer instead of water because" – she paused as she shrugged and threw her hands in the air – "they were lazy?"

Everyone laughed.

"Or maybe they were just tired," she said. "They had to walk all the way to the pump in the center of town for water, but the beer was right here. So St. Arnold ordered everyone in town to drink beer, saving many, many lives."

"Why did that work?" asked the young woman who had been in front of Birdie's mom in the ticket line. Her accent was Spanish and her English was perfect.

"Oh, yes, well, to make beer is like making tea, except you steep grains in boiling water rather than tea leaves. Boiling killed the plague bacteria in the water, making the beer safe to drink. So you see, our dear St. Arnold saved Bruges."

"Did the workers walk around drunk all the time?" Ben asked.

"Some, maybe, who knows?" Elsa wobbled in her heavy-duty black work shoes as if she'd had a few too many. "But most didn't. They had one glass with breakfast, one with lunch and one with dinner, but it was a very mild beer. There was barely any alcohol in it at all. You couldn't do that now with the higher potency brews."

"Definitely not," Uncle Noah said.

"Yes, he knows." Elsa pointed at him. "Any other questions before we move on?"

Hearing none, she led them up a spiral staircase that emptied onto a catwalk suspended three stories above the floor. It swayed under their weight as they crossed into a makeshift museum. Old-fashioned brewing equipment stood in each corner and yellowed photographs hung on the brick walls.

"And here," Elsa announced as she grabbed a metal handle, "is a door to nowhere."

Steamy sunlight flooded the room as she slid a massive wooden door along its track. It opened to an uneasy sky and a steep drop.

"This is where workmen loaded the grains," Elsa explained. "They used their muscles and mechanical hoists to drag the heavy bags up from the wagons below."

Ben stepped to the edge of the opening and peered down.

"Quite a drop." He teetered momentarily before Elsa silently guided him back to the group. He merged in next to his uncle and offered that funny crooked smile.

Uncle Noah did not smile back.

CHAPTER SEVEN

"Time to move on," Elsa said, leading them higher into the brewery.

Birdie followed Ben up a second spiral staircase, this one even narrower than the first. Her sneakers hung halfway off the angled rungs, so she turned her feet to climb sideways. She stayed back so she wouldn't get knocked in the teeth if one of Ben's shoes slipped.

"Whoa. Check this out." He shielded his eyes as he climbed out onto a broad, flat roof, where puddles steamed in the sun. "Looks cool from up here, doesn't it?"

A carpet of red gabled roofs tumbled out far below, with sparkling canals weaving between them like ribbons in a tapestry. Tourist boats drifted along, following a loop that showed off the purple pansies and pink petunias in the window boxes that adorned even the most modest buildings. Sleek windmills rotated in the distance.

"It looks nothing like where I live in Texas," Ben said,

following Birdie's gaze across the rooftops. "Except for the windmills. We've got those. But the rest of the town is like a fairy tale."

From this angle they were eye-level with the steeples and bell towers that rose all over town, serving as guideposts in the confusion of the streets. People were jammed into a handful of the lanes, and the crowd thickened as it neared the Markt.

"Everybody is smooshed together. If they walked a couple of blocks that way" – Birdie pointed toward a quiet curve of lane – "they'd have the whole town to themselves."

"No time for that. Gotta check off the must-do list in the Marty McEntire book."

She laughed. "I guess. I can't talk, though. We were down there earlier, too, eating the fries Marty recommended."

"*Oh, des frites,*" Ben said, adopting a French accent. "*Magnifique!*"

"They were pretty good."

"They're awesome. Best lunch yet. Did you go for the classic Belgian version with mayonnaise?"

"I stuck with plain and tried a little curry ketchup."

"Yeah, I went for the ones with beef gravy. You should try them."

An older woman pushed past them, trailing behind her grandson. She caught him around the middle, then lifted him into her arms as he squirmed to get away. A metal handrail encircled the roof, although it looked as if it were more for show than to keep anyone from falling.

Ben stepped forward and grabbed the railing, leaning over it at the waist. Birdie suppressed an urge to grab his arm and pull him back.

She hovered beside him as she traced the sweep of a canal to a tranquil park with benches and well-manicured flowerbeds. Swans and ducks floated near a towering iron gate at the far end, which opened into a courtyard lined with windswept trees that cast shade across an overgrown lawn. A circle of white bungalows and a faded brick church sat within the tall stone walls.

"That's the Minnewater and the Begijnhof."

"The what and what?"

Ben laughed. "The park is called the Minnewater, and the rest is an old convent called the Begijnhof. It's what Helga was looking for on the map this morning."

"So you knew where it was the whole time?"

The bell in the Markt tolled. Once, twice, three times.

"Better to let them figure it out on their own. Hey, do the bells sound out of tune to you?"

Birdie laughed. She held her wrist so he could see her watch. "They're off by a few minutes too."

"Figures."

Birdie slipped her hands into her pockets and felt the aventurine. She pulled it out and held it up as the sun sparkled off its surface.

"You'd better put it away. Don't want to drop it into the canal."

"What do you think made the gold sparkles move around like that this morning?" She turned it over in her palm before dropping it back into her pocket.

Ben didn't answer right away. "Not sure. Maybe some kind of magnetism?"

"That would mean it isn't gold."

"Then you got me. I've never seen anything like it."

"English tour!" Elsa called across the broad roof. "English tour continues now. We go back down the stairs. Single file and backwards, please!"

Birdie pulled her camera from her daypack and lined up a photo of the park. She could have stayed on the roof all day, watching the tiny people, the flowing water, and the stepped rooftops fanning out into the countryside.

She wrapped her fingers around the warm glass as she concentrated on the memory she was making and the rain-soaked fragrance of the air.

"We have time." Ben sized up the number of people waiting by the stairwell. "They have to crawl down backwards, so it takes a while."

A burst of movement in the park caught her eye. "Hey, look."

"What?"

"Down there."

She pointed to a ragged-looking boy wearing a dark cap and a brown coat. He darted across the green expanse in bare feet, then dipped behind a thick tree at the edge of the park and crouched low. He shimmered in the heat rising from the wet earth.

"He's hiding from somebody," Ben said as he leaned against the railing.

The boy peeked around the knobby trunk but quickly crouched back down.

"I think it's her." Birdie pointed to a stern-looking woman lumbering across the bridge. She was draped in a black robe and wore a broad hood lined with a white scarf that hugged her cheeks. She scanned the park, her irritation clear from the set of her shoulders.

The woman cupped her hands around her mouth and called out, but Birdie and Ben were up too high to make out what she said.

"She's a nun." Ben bent over the railing to get a better look. "Or else she's dressed up like one for the tourists."

"She's got to be hot."

"They do reenactments sometimes. Kind of like Colonial Williamsburg, but from the Middle Ages."

"How do you know all this?"

Ben stood up. "I read the guidebook."

The boy scuffled further behind the tree. It hid him from the nun, even though Birdie could see him perfectly.

And, she realized, he could see her. She took a step back. "He sees us."

The boy placed his finger to his lips.

"Did you see that?"

"Wonder what he did. That nun looks mad as a rattler."

"I wonder if he—"

"Ben! Let's go!"

Ben and Birdie jumped at his name. They turned in time to see the crown of Uncle Noah's head disappear down the stairwell. Birdie realized too late that everyone else was already off the roof.

Ben's shoulders slumped. "Gotta go."

"We both do." Birdie dared one last glance down at the Minnewater. "Hey, wait. They're gone."

"What?" Ben was already several steps away.

"The boy and the nun. They're not there anymore."

"No way." He took a step back toward the railing.

"Ben! Now!" Uncle Noah's voice floated up from the stairwell.

"You'd better go," Birdie said. "Come on."

Ben followed Birdie down the stairs into the cool darkness, climbing backward as everyone else had done. When they landed on the floor, they followed the murmur of voices through a doorway that resembled a porthole and entered the next room. Elsa was talking about a series of stone casks protruding from the walls.

Uncle Noah stood close to Elsa, listening intently. Every so often, he turned an analytical eye toward the ancient equipment.

Birdie spotted her mom a few feet away from him and made her way across the low-ceilinged room.

"There you are. I was wondering where you got to. Hi, Ben."

"So now," Elsa said, "fun time starts. After all those steps, you need a drink, no? Well, you get one now, for free!"

Birdie looked at Mrs. Blessing, who shook her head "no" almost imperceptibly.

After a warm show of gratitude and a round of applause, the tour group bid Elsa goodbye. As she left, she directed them down another set of stairs that led to the sprawling tasting room.

"Enjoy our best Bruges beer," she called, "and don't forget about the gift shop!"

A fresh clap of thunder detonated outside, so close it

made Birdie jump. The collective gasp of the tour group echoed in the spiral stairwell, followed by nervous laughter.

"I guess we'll get that drink after all," her mom said, as rain pelted the brick tower that surrounded them. "I'm sure they have something other than beer."

CHAPTER EIGHT

"They're looser about drinking here than we are at home," her mom explained as she waved off Birdie's beer and ordered a hot chocolate instead. "The drinking ages are younger and kids learn to drink with their parents. It would be unusual for a kid your age to sit down with a beer, though, even here. The bartender probably wasn't paying attention."

"Maybe he thought you wanted it."

"One is more than enough." She held up an enormous glass of golden beer as foam slopped down the sides.

Birdie grabbed a handful of napkins as they exited the far end of the bar.

Ben was waiting for them. "Hey, do y'all want to sit together?"

His uncle was already settled near a roaring fire at the far end of the tasting room. He was scrolling through his cell phone, a tall beer perched in front of him.

Mrs. Blessing looked doubtful. "Oh, I don't—"

"Sure. Let's do it."

Mrs. Blessing raised her eyebrows at her daughter.

"What? All the other tables are full. And check out that fire."

They followed Ben across the tasting room and slid into high-backed chairs near the stone hearth.

"Look who I found, Uncle Noah."

"Hmmm?" He didn't bother to look up. After a beat of silence, he lifted his gaze from the phone. He shook his dark hair away from his eyes when it registered that other people had joined them. "Oh, hey, how are you? You're from the B and B, right?"

"Yes, we met this morning," Mrs. Blessing said. "We arrived last night." She looked like she wanted to begin introductions, but Uncle Noah resumed scrolling.

"How about that rain?" Birdie said, breaking through the awkward silence. "We got in here just in time to avoid getting drenched, and now it's pouring again."

"I wish it would stop," Ben said. "That was our third tour. Hope we don't need another."

"Three?" Mrs. Blessing said.

Ben nodded. "We had three different tour guides. Elsa was the best, so y'all lucked out."

"You must have a lot of questions," Birdie said.

"That I do." Uncle Noah made a final swipe before setting the phone screen-side down on the table. He sipped what Birdie assumed was his third beer. "But I think they're all answered now."

"Thank God." Ben slumped back against his chair.

Uncle Noah took another sip and set his glass down on a

colorful coaster that showcased the brewery's jester mascot.

"So, now you know my story," he said. "What brings you here?"

"Not the beer," Mrs. Blessing said, setting her glass down.

"Hot chocolate's pretty good." Birdie cradled the mug in her hands.

"Oh, that's not what I meant. The beer tastes good. It tastes great, actually. This just isn't the kind of place I'd normally take you to." She turned to Ben's uncle. "We popped in because of the rain and then took the tour. I saw some interesting old equipment, so it was worthwhile."

"I'm glad we came here," Birdie said. "The tour was okay and the view from the roof was amazing. How lucky was it that it stopped raining while we were up there?"

"Why are you interested in old brewing equipment?" Uncle Noah asked.

"It's not the brewing equipment specifically. I'm a designer. I'm always on the lookout for interesting items. I'm studying medieval architecture and decorative arts for a new line of clothing and home accessories."

Uncle Noah didn't seem to have a response to that, so he turned to Birdie. "What grade are you in?"

"Ninth, going into tenth."

"Same as Ben." He leaned back. "Well, we think."

Ben ran his fingers through his messy crop of hair. "Yeah, I'll make it. I'm almost done with the stupid report."

"Better be." He picked his phone back up and resumed scrolling.

"Maybe if we didn't hang out in breweries all day, I'd get more done."

Uncle Noah lifted his eyes from his phone. "Watch it."

"Okay, well, then. This has been fun." Mrs. Blessing checked her watch before remembering that she wasn't wearing one. "How are you coming with that hot chocolate?"

"Almost done. But I want to check out the gift shop before we leave."

Her mom settled back in the chair and picked up a trifold flyer that stood in the center of the table. She began to read it as she waited for Birdie to finish, but then seemed to think better of it.

"I'm going outside to see if the rain has stopped." She took a last sip of beer, then stood and slipped her purse over her shoulder. "I want to sketch the old porch and courtyard."

"Okay, I'll meet you out there. I'm almost done."

Mrs. Blessing paused as if she were going to say goodbye to Ben's uncle, but she turned to Birdie instead. "See you out there."

"Gift shop?" Ben pushed his chair away from the table. "Let's do it."

"Don't be long," Uncle Noah said without looking up.

They zigzagged through the tasting room to the store. The crowd was gone, leaving a few stragglers mingling by the racks. Birdie made a beeline for the bins, with Ben close behind.

"There must be a thousand pieces of aventurine in there," she said.

"Did you read the legend?" Ben pointed to a gold-

lettered sign above the bin that read MAGISCH VENETIAANS
AVENTURINE.

Birdie moved closer to the sign, where the legend
unfurled in Dutch, followed by a French translation. The
English translation was in small print underneath:

*In the early days of Bruges, when its seaport served as a major
center of trade and commerce, goods from all over the world flowed
through town on their way to destinations in Europe. Dutch, French,
and English mingled to create the language of business. Mysterious
sailors from distant lands arrived daily, bringing spices, silks, and
amazing inventions to sell at the Markt.*

*In 1498, an Italian ship arrived in port after a harrowing journey
from Venice. It carried hundreds of miniature boxes crafted from a rare
wood with blue and gold marbling. The ornate boxes created such a
sensation that all were sold in less than a day. Every wealthy home in
Bruges and beyond soon coveted a box for its mantel.*

*Long after the Italian ship returned to sea, a well-respected lace
merchant in Bruges discovered a secret chamber in the bottom of his box.
Inside, three oval jewels shimmered. They were quite unusual: Golden
sparkles swirled on the surface of each one, forming simple shapes. The
man didn't know the jewels were composed of a mysterious Venetian
glass called aventurine, but he soon learned that each shape that formed
opened a window to the past.*

"A window to the past?" Birdie locked eyes with Ben.
"Keep going."
She continued, reading the last part aloud.

As word spread of the magical glass, people journeyed from far and wide for a glimpse of days gone by. The merchant welcomed any who could pay a fee into his home to see the glass. He put his children to work guiding the seekers as they slipped between visions of the past and the stark reality of the present day.

But as autumn turned to winter, whispers emerged that those who had touched the aventurine were falling ill, and rumors raced across Bruges that the merchant had unleashed the plague. The church accused the man of heresy, a crime punishable by death. The priests confiscated the pieces of aventurine, then took them to the Basilica of the Holy Blood, where they were never seen again.

The merchant and his family fled Bruges in the night.
No one knows what became of them.

Birdie finished reading the legend and glanced around the brightly lit gift shop. "Holy crap."

"Some legend, eh?"

"Talk about bad luck. Maybe I'll leave it on the windowsill for the next kid."

"It's kinda weird that they made a toy commemorating some poor family that got run out of town." He pointed to the bottom of the sign. "And it costs a whole whopping euro."

He grabbed a piece of aventurine from the bin and turned it over in his hand. He rubbed a round section on the back and a picture of a door materialized, formed from what looked like gold glitter.

He raised his eyebrows. "It's different from the one in your pocket."

Something looked off to Birdie, too, as she watched Ben rub the toy.

She reached down and picked one up from the bin.

"Oh," she breathed.

It wasn't a piece of glass at all. It was made of hard rubber, like the windmills and other toys. The place where the picture formed was a bubble sticker with gold glitter inside.

"What?" Ben tossed the toy back into the bin. It bounced around as it hit the others, then settled against its twins.

"You're right. It's not the same. The piece of glass I found. It's not like these. It's not a toy."

"I bet the brewery's not the only place trying to make a buck off the legend. Yours could be from one of the expensive gift shops on the Markt."

"The glass is completely different."

"Ben!"

Birdie glanced up and saw Uncle Noah charging across the shop. She rolled her eyes. "Is he always like this?"

Ben blew out a sigh. "Always. I gotta go."

"Yeah. See you later."

Most folks enjoy a meal at an outside table at the
Market Square, watching all the action. I recommend
stepping off the main drag and visiting a smaller, locally run
establishment where they're less likely to speak your language
and more likely to have food you'll remember.

—*Marty McEntire,* Europe for Americans Travel Guide

CHAPTER NINE

The rest of the day passed quickly. Birdie and her mom returned their bikes to the rental shop, picked up rich chocolates, and relaxed in a courtyard behind a belfry as the carillon played. They had just enough time to drop into the Church of Our Lady before it closed.

"I want to go back to the church again before we leave," her mom said as they settled into a corner table at a café a few blocks from t'Bruges Huis. It was almost eight o'clock and Birdie's stomach was rumbling.

"Why?"

"That statue. The Madonna and Child. It was gorgeous. So peaceful. And the details in the church were exquisite."

"You want to sketch."

"I want to sketch. There wasn't enough time to do more than admire the statue. I want to study it."

A willowy waitress in a plaid shirt took their order. The menu was short and showcased different versions of toasted cheese sandwiches, with or without a salad. Birdie ordered spaghetti with meat sauce, which looked like the most filling item on the menu. Her mom picked a toasted ham and cheese sandwich with a salad.

When the waitress left, her mom leaned on her elbows and looked deep into Birdie's hazel eyes. "How are you holding up, kiddo?"

Her mom didn't have to explain what she meant. She wasn't talking about the long day of sightseeing, or Birdie's tired feet, or the whisper of jet lag that still lingered.

"I'm okay."

The truth was, she'd been okay all afternoon. More than okay. She'd had fun exploring the town and hanging out with Ben. Her heart sank when she realized she hadn't thought of Jonah once, not even when she was eating *des frites*. He'd loved fries.

"I…" She couldn't continue. She turned to the window and watched people walking by without really seeing them. The crowds had thinned as the day wore on, departing by bus to return to the tourist hotels in the bigger cities.

"What is it, Birdie?"

She didn't dare turn back to her mom. If she did, she wouldn't be able to keep the tears at bay.

"Tell me."

"I feel guilty," she whispered.

Her mom said nothing. She gazed out the window too.

"Here you go," the waitress said several minutes later, settling hot food in front of each of them.

"Thank you," Mrs. Blessing said. When the waitress was out of earshot, she said, "Come on, now, you need to eat."

Birdie nodded. She took a deep breath and focused on

the spaghetti, which was hot and, despite her sadness, tasted good.

They ate in silence – both of them hungry and tired, and neither of them keen to talk about what they'd left behind. It wasn't until they'd finished eating and a steaming cup of hot chocolate sat in front of each of them that Mrs. Blessing spoke again.

"I feel guilty too. Every time I smile or go for hours concentrating on something else."

"I don't want to forget, and sometimes I do, Mom." Birdie wrinkled her nose to keep the tears from welling in her eyes. "I forget for a little while and then when I remember again, I feel awful inside. Like they'll think I don't love them anymore."

"They know you love them." Her mom reached across the table and took her hand. "They know we love them. I don't think they'd want us to feel awful forever."

The tears came now. She couldn't stop them. "But I should feel awful forever."

"Why is that?"

"Because it was my fault." Her voice was barely a whisper. "The accident. It was all my fault."

"The accident was not your fault."

She squeezed her eyes closed. "Laurie Billet said it was."
"What?"

"She told the whole bus that Dad and Jonah would never have died if I hadn't wanted them at my dance recital. And she's right, Mom. If they would've stayed for Jonah's second game, if they hadn't left the double-header to get to the auditorium in time—"

"Birdie. Look at me."

She opened her eyes and saw the yellow fire in her mother's hazel ones.

"Laurie Billet is an awful girl who knows nothing about anything. You know very well that your father and your brother wanted to come to that recital. In fact, Jonah begged your dad to leave the game early."

"He did?"

"He did. He wanted to see you, of course, but he also wanted to see Melanie. Do you remember Melanie?"

"Oh." She exhaled as the realization sunk in. "He wanted to go out with her. I heard him talking to Trevor about it."

"That's right. And your dad? Your dad wanted to see you. He felt guilty too. He managed to make it to every single one of Jonah's baseball games and yet always seemed to be out of town when you had something special going on. When was the last time he went to one of your school concerts?"

She thought about it. "I don't remember."

"Exactly. So don't beat yourself up because the accident happened on the way to the recital. If your dad or Jonah had insisted the other way – that they stay at the game – you'd have understood. It's not like you were throwing a tantrum to get them there."

"I was so glad they were coming, though. My routine was so cool."

"I know it was, kiddo."

They'd never seen the routine. They'd never made it off the turnpike. They'd left the game in plenty of time, even with the slowed traffic from the bridge construction. But it didn't matter. The truck driver behind them was asleep. He never even hit the brakes.

Mrs. Blessing dug in her purse and handed her a small packet of tissues. "It's different here. I admit that. At home, there were reminders everywhere, especially with all the packing. Here there are very few."

Birdie had tried to forget about the packing. Although a grief counselor had suggested that someone else collect her dad and Jonah's things to donate to charity, they hadn't listened. They'd packed every belonging themselves, even the old socks with sagging elastic they found in the back of one of her dad's drawers, and the Transformers Jonah had hidden under his bed so his friends wouldn't see them.

And they'd given nothing to charity.

As she wiped her eyes and blew her nose, a memory drifted back, as clear as if it were happening again. She'd come home from school to find her mom sitting on Jonah's bedroom floor, in the same place she'd been when she left that morning, next to a cardboard box half-filled with his clothes. She was clasping an old T-shirt to her chest and staring out his window at the swing set, lost in another day, another memory.

Birdie had taken the shirt from her hands, helped her to her feet and out of the bedroom. She'd settled her downstairs on the couch where she could curl up and cry like she'd done so many nights after the accident. Birdie had warmed up a can of soup for dinner and then climbed back upstairs to finish packing Jonah's clothes.

That box was tucked away with all the others now, labeled with a black marker and stacked in the dark storage unit back home.

And they were here.

And her mother was no longer crying.

"What will we do when we go back?" Part of her didn't want to know, didn't care, didn't really want to go back at all.

"To be honest, I'm not sure."

"Where will we live?"

Her mom shrugged.

"Will we be homeless?"

"No, of course not." She dismissed the question with a shake of her head. "I suppose we'll move back to our house if it doesn't sell, although it's much too big for us. We might buy a place in town or rent an apartment."

"So we're going back to Bamburg?"

"I think so. I don't want to pull you from a school where you have friends."

Birdie would have been okay leaving her school, but her mom didn't know that.

"We'll see how things go. We're here for the entire summer, and this is only our second day. I'm hoping our future will become clearer as our trip continues."

"That doesn't sound like you."

"No, I suppose it doesn't."

"You're kind of a planner, Mom."

"I'm a big planner. I had our whole life planned. But the universe had different ideas. And now... Well, now I need to let go and see what happens."

After they finished the hot chocolate, they made their way along the cobblestone lanes to t'Bruges Huis. It was still light out, even though it was nearly ten o'clock. Birdie avoided looking up at the surrounding windows. She was glad the summer days here were so long.

Mrs. Blessing punched the code into the glowing green panel, and the stately wooden door clicked open. Birdie followed her inside, tripping the automatic sensor for the chandelier and flooding the foyer with light.

A crash that sounded like glass hitting glass came from the sitting room.

Birdie took a step forward and looked through the archway.

A teenage girl with long blond hair and startled blue eyes stared back at her.

"Oh, hello." She sat up quickly. Definitely American. "Sorry about the noise. I just dropped my phone."

The phone in question had landed on the coffee table near a curvy carafe half-full of golden liquid. A puddle from an overturned glass was flowing toward the phone.

"You'd better grab it," Birdie said, pointing to the coming disaster.

"Right." The girl retrieved the phone and then collapsed back onto the love seat. She gave the screen a once-over to make sure it was okay.

"Are you Kayla?" Mrs. Blessing followed Birdie into the sitting room. "We met your grandparents this morning at breakfast."

Kayla stopped fiddling with her phone. "Yes, that's me. Are you the Blessings? They mentioned you too."

"That's us." Mrs. Blessing glanced around the sitting room. "Is anyone else here?"

"My grandparents are in bed already. Mrs. Devon only comes out in the morning. I'm not sure that she lives here, actually. I don't know about the other guests – those guys from Texas? I haven't seen them all day. In fact, I haven't seen them at all. Just heard them walking by the room." She stopped short, as if she realized she was rambling.

"Okay, then, it was nice to meet you, Kayla. We've had a big day exploring, so we're off to bed too." Mrs. Blessing paused before she continued. "I think I saw clean towels on the shelf in the dining room if you need to wipe that up."

Kayla's face went a shade paler. "Okay, um, thanks."

Birdie used the last of her energy to climb the stairs to the attic bedroom. She changed into her pajamas and settled in to bed.

"Why do you think she doesn't want to be with her grandparents?" she asked as her mom headed toward the bathroom. "They seemed nice to me."

"I don't know." She met Birdie's eyes. "But one thing I've learned is that there's always more to things than you think."

CHAPTER TEN

The next morning dawned brightly as the last whisper of the evening's storms drifted east with the wind. Willy reclaimed the windowsill in a regal display of gray and white feathers, bobbing his head to the room before calling to his companions across the sleepy city.

"Morning, Willy." Birdie snuggled deeper into the cocoon of her yellow duvet. "Thanks for the wake-up call."

She wished she could stay in bed longer, watching Willy and gazing at the sun breaking over the rooftops across the street. But it was not to be. Her mom had already left the room, which meant she was probably late for breakfast.

The thought of missing Mrs. Devon's wonderful cooking provided the burst of energy she needed to climb out of bed.

She showered and dressed before joining her mom in the dining room, where she sat alone studying a tiny porcelain bowl. She turned it over in her hands and read something etched on the bottom.

"Morning." Birdie slid into the same chair she'd sat in the

day before.

"Good morning." Mrs. Blessing set the bowl next to her plate. "How did you sleep?"

"Good."

"No dreams?"

"None that I remember."

"Good." Her mom plucked the white linen napkin from her plate, where it stood like a three-cornered hat. She shook it and placed it across her lap.

The tiered serving tray in the center of the table was artfully arranged with breads, pastries, jellies, jams, and small jars of plain white yogurt. Birdie reached for a yogurt and a tiny container of raspberry preserves.

A rumble on the stairs signaled Ben's arrival.

"Howdy." He crossed through the sitting room and folded into the seat next to Birdie. He reached for two pieces of cinnamon-nut bread and the butter dish.

"Good morning, Ben," Mrs. Blessing said.

"So what did y'all do last night?" He used a small knife to apply a thick layer of butter to the bread.

"We met Kayla," Birdie said.

"Really? I was beginning to wonder if she existed." He bit a hunk off the cinnamon-nut bread.

"Oh, she exists alright," Harry said as he lumbered across the sitting area. "She's just in a different time zone than the rest of us."

He took a seat across the table from Mrs. Blessing.

The door swung open and Mrs. Devon emerged from the kitchen. "Good morning, everyone." She bustled around the table as she poured coffee. "Would anyone care for an egg?"

"That would be wonderful," Mrs. Blessing said. "What about you two?"

Birdie opted for a boiled egg with toast and Ben asked for a three-egg omelet.

"Cheese?"

"Yes, ma'am."

"And toast, I think?"

Ben nodded. Mrs. Devon smiled warmly and returned to the kitchen.

"Any big plans for today?" Harry asked.

"It looks like a great day for the canal cruise."

Harry nodded his approval and then, although her mom had not requested it, launched into a detailed explanation of the procedure for finding the dock, buying the tickets, and boarding the boat.

Ben leaned in close. "Do you have the aventurine?"

She retrieved it from the front pocket of her jeans and rubbed its smooth surface with her thumb. As she did, the golden flakes shimmered and moved.

"Whoa," he said under his breath. "It's doing it again."

Birdie handed the piece of glass to Ben. His breath caught when he touched it. "It's getting warm."

"It's nothing like those toys at the brewery."

"What's it making?" He balanced the glass on his open palm under the table between them. The sparkles quickened and took shape. They collided into streams of golden light, swirling and undulating before driving together into a perfect image.

"Holy crow, that's hot." He dropped the aventurine on the seat beside him and rubbed his hand on his cargo shorts.

He examined the newly formed picture on the glass. "What is that?"

"It looks kind of like a knight," she said, as surprised as Ben sounded. "You know, from a chess set?"

"Do you play chess?"

"I never learned. But my brother had a chess set in his room at home. He and my dad—"

"You have a brother?" Ben raised his eyebrows in surprise.

She realized too late that she had said too much.
"I—"

"What do you two have there?" Her mom leaned around her to see what was sitting on the seat next to Ben.

"It's a toy," they both said at once. They looked at each other.

Ben laughed. "You owe me a pop."

Birdie covered the aventurine with her hand. It had cooled enough to handle, and she slipped it back into her pocket.

"What's so funny?" Helga asked as she made her way across the sitting room and took the seat next to her husband. As she did, Mrs. Devon returned with an egg in a dainty cup for Birdie and, for Ben, an omelet so large that its edges slipped over the sides of the plate.

"For you. *Bon appétit.*"

With Helga's arrival, the conversation shifted back to plans for the day. Even Ben seemed distracted from his question by the size of the steaming breakfast before him.

Birdie poked at her egg, which was sitting upright, still in its shell. A spoon so small that a sugar cube would dwarf it sat on the flowered saucer under the cup. She picked up the tiny spoon and knocked it into the top of the egg, but nothing happened. She whacked it again, but it still didn't crack.

"Should've got an omelet." Ben speared his fork into a hunk of egg and cheese.

"Do you have plans for dinner tonight?" Helga extracted a large fruit and cheese danish from the middle tier of the serving rack.

"Not yet," Birdie's mom said.

"You could join us if you'd like. Couldn't they, Harry? We'd love the company. We're going to the oldest pub in town. It's called Herberg-something. It's about half a kilometer away – right, Harry?"

He nodded. He, too, had opted for the three-egg omelet and was enjoying it wholeheartedly.

"Marty says it's an easy walk," Helga continued. "And it's supposed to make you feel like you went back in time. It celebrated its five hundredth anniversary a few years ago."

"What do you think, Birdie?" her mom asked.

"Okay by me." She had not yet succeeded in removing the egg from its shell.

"Oh, that's good. Let's plan to meet in the sitting room at 6:30 – I'm sorry, I mean 18:30 – and we can all walk over together." Helga turned to Ben. "You're welcome to join us, too, and your uncle, of course."

"Thank you, ma'am." He sounded doubtful. "I'll ask."

Birdie set the useless spoon back on the saucer and picked up a large, heavy butter knife from beside her plate.

Crack!

That did it: the weight of the knife dented the shell. She used her fingers to remove the chalky white fragments and then carefully cut the egg open with the knife.

"Mom."

Mrs. Blessing paused halfway through a sentence and looked over at her.

"Oh, that's okay. It's soft-boiled. Just dip some toast in there."

Birdie glanced at Ben.

He shrugged. "Should've got the omelet."

CHAPTER ELEVEN

After breakfast, Birdie and her mom wandered through sunny cobblestone lanes until they stumbled upon a wobbly wooden dock where a line was already forming for the next canal cruise. They bought two tickets and joined the rest of the tourists as they waited for the narrow boat to dock and unload its passengers.

Her mom leaned in close and nodded toward the teenage boy piloting the canal boat. "Is he old enough to be the captain?"

Birdie tilted her head for a better view. He wasn't much older than she was, with clipped blond hair and a golden tan. "He's cute. Besides, it'll be fine. The canals are skinny and we can always swim to shore."

"Hilarious." Mrs. Blessing stepped forward, beaming at the handsome young captain as he reached up to help her onto the boat. Birdie rolled her eyes and followed, squeezing onto a long bench between the other passengers.

She shoved the ticket stub into her pocket, and her fingers

brushed the aventurine. She dug it out and turned it over in her hand. The gold wasn't moving anymore, and the chess piece held firm as she rubbed it.

The open craft jerked sideways as two men shoved it from the dock, then jostled under the weight of its passengers before evening out in the middle of the canal. Birdie slipped her hands into her jacket pockets before the aventurine could fly into the canal.

As the boat settled, the captain fired up the engine, and they crawled through the languid water. He recited a well-rehearsed script through a crackly speaker, first in Dutch, then in French, and finally in English.

After the first few trilingual explanations, Birdie tuned him out and studied the view of the medieval city from this lower angle, spotting the docks and the delivery doors that backed up to the water.

"Duck!" the captain yelled as they neared a low stone bridge. They all bent low in the boat as they passed through the darkness. They floated back into the sun and rounded a bend by a different dock jammed with tourists waiting for the next cruise.

Birdie spotted some boys playing in a patch of grass a few yards beyond the stone wall that lined the canal. They were dressed as if they were going to one of the historical reenactments Ben had told her about.

They were playing some kind of game, hurling rocks at a stake in the ground. As the boat drifted closer to the bank, Birdie realized it wasn't a stake at all, but a bird buried so only its head stuck out from the dirt.

She gasped and twisted away. "Mom, did you…"

"They all give the same tour," her mom said, oblivious to the grisly game being played on the canal bank. She leaned close so the captain wouldn't hear. "The city regulates how much they charge and what they can say. That's what Marty says, anyway."

Birdie lost sight of the boys as the boat made a wide U-turn.

Had she seen what she thought she did? Who would do that?

She watched for the grassy patch after their turn, but when they passed by it again, there was no trace of the boys – just a handful of tourists wandering through.

Were her eyes playing tricks on her? Perhaps she'd imagined the boys or misinterpreted what she saw. Who would do such a terrible thing to a bird?

She thought of Willy, bobbing his head on the windowsill that morning.

It must have been a toy. It was the only explanation that made sense. The tourists would have intervened if they saw the boys hurting a poor defenseless bird.

She settled against the hard bench and closed her eyes for a moment to push the image from her mind. Then she took a deep breath of humid air and opened them again.

As they approached the bridge, she noticed a sandy-haired boy with an odd-looking hat leaning over the side. The sun's reflection off the water made him shimmer, and he seemed to stare right at her.

As they drew closer, she realized she recognized him. It was the same boy they'd seen from the brewery roof. He wore the same dark cap and heavy clothes. Behind him, a horse pulled a tourist carriage with an elderly couple perched in the back.

He was definitely staring at her.

Birdie waved.

He waved back.

The boat had almost reached the bridge when his smile faltered. He turned his head as if he'd heard a loud sound. She checked the bridge to see what distracted him, but nothing seemed obvious.

Suddenly, he sprinted away on bare feet, disappearing into the thickening crowd.

"Wait!" she cried, half-standing.

"Birdie! Sit down!" Her mom grabbed her jacket and pulled her back into the boat. "You'll get your head knocked off by the bridge. What are you thinking?"

"I…" she began, but the captain's monotone narrative drowned her out as he continued in a language she didn't understand. He paused and switched to English.

"On the right side…"

Birdie hunkered down and scanned the canal bank for the boy.

There was no sign of him.

The boat slowed when they reached another broad intersection and then reversed course, heading back the way they'd come.

She almost stood again when she caught sight of the boy a few moments later, leaping up the front steps of a red brick house with purple and red blooms tumbling from its window boxes. He slid through a sliver of open door and was gone.

She twisted in her seat to watch the house as they passed.

A tabby cat wove a lazy circle on the stoop and sat down. Someone had drawn the curtains tight behind the window boxes on each floor, except for a single window under the eaves, where they were open wide.

A little girl peered down from the window, her palm pressing the glass. She stood steadfast in her high-collared blouse, making it hard to tell if she was real or a well-placed portrait.

Birdie blinked. The girl was still there, but as she watched, she faded back into the room like a shadow.

The canal boat sounded its horn, a crass beep that startled everyone on board.

It didn't matter, anyway. The house was behind them now, out of sight around the bend.

Birdie sighed as she settled back onto the crowded bench and waited for the cruise to end.

CHAPTER TWELVE

"What did you see back there?" her mom asked as they made their way off the dock. "You scared the heck out of me."

"Sorry. I saw a boy. He waved to me."

"Was it Ben?"

"No, someone local, I think. He was younger than Ben and dressed in heavy clothes. We saw him yesterday from the brewery roof too. I think he's one of the historical reenactors."

"Ah. I read something about that." She frowned. "Only…"

"What?'

"I thought Marty said they did that in the fall, as part of a heritage festival." She shook her head. "It doesn't matter. But it does explain why it took you so long to rejoin the tour."

When Birdie didn't respond, her mom said, "Maybe you could sketch him."

She stopped walking. "That's a good idea. But—"

"There." Her mom pointed to a shaded green bench close to the bridge where the boy had stood. "We could sit there for a while."

"But I'm not sure I can draw him."

"You won't know unless you try."

They made their way through the crowded street to the empty bench and sat down.

Birdie tugged her sketchbook from her daypack and opened it wide across her lap. She pointed her toes against the cobblestones to level the book on her legs, then turned to a crisp, blank page. She picked out colored pencils that most closely matched her impression of the boy, the sandy hair and dark coat, the pale skin and dirt-stained shirt.

To her surprise and relief, the drawing came easily, as if she were sketching from somewhere deep inside to conjure his image. In the picture, he stood on the bridge with one bare foot resting on the stone curb, his face lit with a slight smile as he stared at something in the distance.

When she was done, she placed the last pencil in the pouch and considered her work.

It was the best picture of a living, breathing human being she'd ever sketched.

"No shoes?" Her mom took a break from her own sketch to study Birdie's drawing.

She shook her head and closed the sketchbook on his toes.

"You don't have to stop."

"I'm done for now." She leaned over and looked at her mom's work. "What are you drawing?"

Mrs. Blessing pointed down the canal to an arched window towering above the doors of a cathedral. It was several blocks away, but Birdie could make out the scrolled metal work that had caught her attention.

"Nice."

"It's okay." She closed her sketchbook too. "I need to spend more time drawing to capture what I'm seeing. I feel like I never spend more than a few minutes on anything. There are so many distractions everywhere." She pulled her camera from her purse, zoomed in, and took a photo of the window.

"Like that." She pointed to the place she'd just photographed. "I keep finding these interesting arches and windows. I'm just not capturing them very well. And the photos don't do them justice. I feel like I need to get one right before I move on to other things."

"We could go back to Mrs. Devon's and you could do some drawing before dinner," Birdie said.

"You wouldn't mind?"

"No."

"But there are so many more things to see." She rummaged in her purse. "Marty McEntire listed—"

"Mom, it's okay." She touched her mom's hand. "Really."

Mrs. Blessing dropped the guidebook back into her purse. "I do like the idea of an afternoon of drawing."

"Isn't that why we're here? So you can come up with designs?"

"That's why we're here."

"Let's go then."

Back at t'Bruges Huis, the sitting room held the still air of solitude that settled on an empty house.

"We can eat at the table," her mom said, lifting the bag of sandwiches they'd picked up at a café on the way back to the bed-and-breakfast.

It was eerie, eating at the table without the companionship of the other guests, and they finished quickly. Afterward, Mrs. Blessing sat on the love seat in the sitting room and placed her materials on the end table beside her, while Birdie settled into a high-backed chair and propped her feet up on the coffee table.

"Birdie, please."

"Fine." She lowered her sneakers and opened her sketchbook to the page with the boy.

He stared back at her, his smile wide, his old-fashioned pants hiding skinny ankles.

Who was he?

She selected pencils in two shades of brown and filled in more details – the dirt on his feet, the creases in his billowy white shirt.

The house was silent except for the scratching of her mother's charcoal on the porous paper and the slow tick of the grandfather clock that loomed against the wall. Sunlight pooled on the floor then disappeared as clouds passed by outside.

"Hey?" Birdie asked a long while later, when she'd done as much work as she could on the sketch without ruining it.

"Hmmm?"

"Do you feel like going for a walk?"

Her mom didn't look up from the page. "Not right now, no. I'm kind of in the zone."

Birdie closed her sketchbook and placed it on the table with her pencil pouch. She stood and stretched in front of an enormous fireplace with a hulking marble mantle. Portraits of an unsmiling man and a woman hung on either side. Their dark clothes were enriched with lace collars and sleeves. It was the most uncomfortable-looking clothing she'd ever seen. She couldn't imagine wearing a lace collar the size of a life-preserver around her neck. How could they have possibly thought that was fashionable?

"Let's go."

The front door muffled Uncle Noah's voice, but he was so loud that Birdie heard him clearly. Her mom looked up from her drawing and they exchanged a surprised glance.

"What's your problem?" It was Ben, matching his uncle's volume.

"You're the problem. You need to get your crap together."

"I finished the damned paper, okay? I sent it off last night."

"Late."

"It was not late. I had until tomorrow to get it done."

"It was due back in May."

"I had an extension."

"That's the problem." The door cracked open as Uncle Noah continued, his voice growing louder. "You always expect special treatment."

"I do not." They were in the foyer now, facing off.

Mrs. Blessing cleared her throat.

The effect was immediate.

Uncle Noah stiffened.

"Oh, hey." He turned toward them.

Mrs. Blessing offered a curt nod and returned to her sketch.

Birdie's stomach sank at the look of pure mortification that passed across Ben's face.

Uncle Noah turned back to him and scowled. "I'm going upstairs to get some work done. Unlike you, I don't have an extension. I need to get the business plan done or there won't be a business. That's how it works in the real world."

Ben stood motionless in the foyer, watching his uncle trudge up the stairs. They all heard a door close louder than it should have when he reached the hallway above them.

Ben seemed to debate his next move.

"Do you want to go for a walk?" Birdie made her way across the sitting room and out into the foyer where he stood. He looked like he was about to bolt out the door.

"Yeah." His voice was gruff, and he didn't meet her eyes. "Sure."

"Mom, do you mind?"

She looked up from her sketchbook and sighed. "No, I don't mind. Are you sure your uncle will be okay with it?"

"Who cares?" Ben asked. "Not him."

"You might be wrong there," Mrs. Blessing said.

They stood in silence for several moments.

"Well, go ahead then. Don't be long. We need to get ready for dinner with Helga and Harry in about an hour."

"Thanks, Mom."

"And watch for cars." She touched the charcoal to the

paper. "They drive up these narrow lanes like maniacs."

There are many lovely parks in Bruges to take a break from all the action. One beautiful spot is the Minnewater, a park and "lake of love" near the Begijnhof.

—*Marty McEntire,* Europe for Americans Travel Guide

CHAPTER THIRTEEN

"Are you alright?" Birdie asked after they'd closed the door and made their way to the alley up the street.

"Yeah, I'm alright." He released a pent-up breath as he ran his fingers through his disheveled hair. "My uncle doesn't trust me."

"Oh."

"Yeah."

They walked on without speaking.

They hadn't gone far when they heard a fast rumble behind them. Birdie jumped up onto a tiny curb, pulling Ben up beside her just in time to avoid a small black taxi barreling up the alley.

Ben stepped down onto the cobblestones. "Thanks."

"No problem. It's the second taxi that almost creamed me."

He stopped and met her eyes. "It's my parents."

"In the taxi?"

"No. Not in the taxi." He shook his head and half-smiled.

"My parents are the reason my uncle doesn't trust me. Before they shipped me off with him, they told him I'm a bad kid and I needed to get away from Marshall Falls."

"They really said that?"

Ben didn't reply.

"You didn't want to come?"

"Not really. But now that I'm here, it's kind of cool, you know? Uncle Noah just can't let it go though."

"Didn't he want you to come?"

"He said he did, but, hell, I don't know. He doesn't act like it."

"He seems pretty busy with the brewery thing."

"Yeah."

They'd emerged from the alley by a stone wall overlooking the canal. Ben leaned over the wall and stared into the water.

"Any fish?" Birdie asked.

"I don't see any."

They watched the water for a while as the tourist boats passed beneath them.

"Hey. I didn't get a chance to tell you. I saw that boy again."

Ben stood up. "You did? The one from the brewery?"

"Yep. I saw him when my mom and I were on the canal cruise this morning. He was on a bridge we passed under. And get this, he waved to me."

"No way."

"Way. But then he ran away."

"Which way did he go?" Ben glanced up and down the canal as if the boy would magically appear.

"Uh, well, let me see." She turned in a circle to get her bearings. "We got on the cruise at the other end of town and then traveled past here and up by the church." She pointed to the church at the far end of the bend. "Then we turned around and came back past here. He was on the second bridge, I think. Then he ran off, heading in that direction." She pointed to the other side of the canal bank. "I caught sight of him going into one of the old houses on the waterfront."

"Let's go." Ben started off at a fast clip and she had to jog to catch up to him.

"Where?"

"To his house."

"Why?"

"Why not?"

"I'm not sure I can find it again."

"Well, let's go check it out, anyway."

They followed the canal until they reached the second bridge. As they crossed it, Birdie could hear the narration from the tourist boat passing beneath them.

Ben stopped. "Okay, which way?"

She pointed to the right, and they took off down another cobblestone lane.

She stopped jogging. "This is hopeless. Everything looks the same."

"This isn't it?"

"No, I don't think so."

"Well, hell." He studied the buildings around them as if they'd provide a clue.

"Let's keep going," she said. "Maybe we'll find a hotel or

a bike shop with a map."

They walked to the end of the lane, but didn't see any place that might have a free map. As they neared another intersection, the lane opened into a park with tall trees and a manicured lawn.

A red brick building loomed above it. "It's the brewery," Birdie said. "And this must be the park the boy was in. What did you call it? The Minnewater?"

Ben pointed to a large tree near the canal. "I think that's where he was hiding."

They crossed the park and circled the tree as a tour group explored the top of the brewery, admiring the view of Bruges from the rooftops. Maybe some other kid was up there watching them, although the distance was far enough that she couldn't make out anyone's face in particular. She could tell that some people were shorter than others, and some wore more colorful jackets, while others were dressed in black. But she couldn't make out facial features.

She wondered if the tourists could see her better than she could see them, maybe even as clearly as she'd seen the boy the afternoon before. Perhaps it was a trick of the light and the clouds. She placed her finger to her lips, just as the boy had done, then ducked down, smiling. Now someone else would have a mystery kid to find.

Birdie's smile didn't last long after she turned away from the brewery and examined the space behind the tree.

Under a delicate web of soft leaves and grass clippings lay a package wrapped in paper and twine, barely visible under the greenery. It was small, not much larger than her hand. "What is that?" Ben dropped to one knee to get a better look. He brushed the leaves away and picked up the package. "It's heavy. And a little damp." He glanced up at her. "Think we should open it?"

"It doesn't belong to us."

"So? Finders keepers." He stood, dusting the grass clippings from his knee as he handed her the package. "Open it."

She unwound the twine and pulled the paper wrapping away. "It's a book."

"Let me see."

The volume was bound in deep brown leather and cinched shut with a thin strip of cowhide. The cover held no words, but a knight was embossed on the smooth material.

Birdie recognized it at once. It looked just like the chess piece on the aventurine.

"Whoa," Ben said as she examined the cover. "It looks old."

"It feels old." She handed it to him.

"It must weigh three pounds," he said.

"Do you think it was his?" She fished the aventurine from her pocket and held it next to the book. The images were identical.

"Well, I didn't notice a book when we saw him from the roof, but we were pretty far away. Did he have one when you saw him on the bridge?"

"I don't think so, but that doesn't mean…" She slipped the glass into the pocket of her jeans.

"I know, but it's still interesting." He handed the book back to her.

"It's damp but it's not wet. If he'd dropped it while we

were on the roof, the storm would have soaked it." She replaced the wrapping and secured the twine.

"He had it tucked under those leaves pretty good."

"Still." Birdie cradled it in the crook of her arm. "What do you think we should do with it?"

"Nothing for now." He glanced around to make sure they weren't being watched. The group on the brewery roof had descended the stairs. "Here, wait, give it back to me."

She hesitated.

"Don't you trust me?"

She studied his deep brown eyes for a moment and then handed him the book. He pulled open the Velcro flap on the bottom pocket of his cargo shorts and slipped the book inside. It just fit, although it weighed down the side of his pants.

"That's not obvious," Birdie said.

"No one will be looking for it, so they'll just think I brought a guidebook along."

"Good point." She checked her watch. "Oh crap, we've got to go. Let's take it back to the house and open it."

When they arrived at the bed-and-breakfast, they found a welcome committee waiting for them in the sitting room. Birdie's mom had been joined by Helga and Harry, who were sitting in the armchairs across from her, enjoying a glass of the golden liquid from the carafe that sat in the middle of the coffee table. Kayla, who was clearly not enjoying a glass, was standing near the fireplace, studying her phone.

Uncle Noah was pacing the small room.

"Hey," Birdie said as they came in and the conversation faltered. "Are we late?"

"Where did you go?" Uncle Noah exploded toward Ben.

Mrs. Blessing exchanged glances with Helga and Harry. There was no way out of the sitting room without stepping right between Ben and his uncle.

"For a walk," Ben answered, rising to his full height.

"Mr. Martin." Birdie stepped in front of Ben. "It's my fault. I asked him to go for a walk with me. I was bored, and I asked my mom, but she was busy." She cast a sidelong glance at her mom that said she was sorry for dragging her into this.

"She's telling the truth," Mrs. Blessing said from her place on the love seat. "I told them it was okay."

"What right do you have to tell my nephew what he can and can't do?" Uncle Noah turned on his heel to confront Birdie's mom.

"Now, calm down, son," Harry said.

Mrs. Blessing rose to her feet, lifting a steadying hand to silence Harry.

"You will not speak to me in that tone," she said, her gaze latching onto Uncle Noah's. "You were not here when the decision was being made. My daughter wanted to go for a walk and I trusted your nephew, who has been nothing but courteous and kind to us – which is more than I can say about you, by the way – to accompany her."

Uncle Noah opened his mouth, but no words came. His deep eyes, so fiery a moment before, became unreadable.

The silence stretched.

Even Kayla stopped swiping her phone long enough to

take in the situation.

Birdie held her breath.

"Sorry," Uncle Noah mumbled.

Harry stood and crossed the room. He slapped a thick arm around Uncle Noah's shoulders. "What do you say we head over to the pub early? We can make sure everything's set for dinner before everyone else arrives." He turned to Birdie and Ben. "You kids need to get cleaned up, right? Ben, will you escort the ladies to the pub when they're ready?"

No one said anything.

Birdie considered kicking Ben's sneaker to get him to respond.

Harry looked hard at Ben and raised his bushy eyebrows.

"Yes, sir," Ben mumbled. "Will do."

The tension slipped from the room.

"Very good. We'll see you there." Harry's mustache concealed his upper lip as he nodded his approval.

Uncle Noah and Harry left, saying nothing more. After the door clicked closed, Helga shooed them away with a sweep of her hand. "Well, you heard the man. Go get yourselves together."

Birdie and Ben escaped up the stairs. He paused in front of his door on the first landing.

"I'm sorry," she whispered, feeling guilty that she'd asked him to take the walk with her.

"Do you want the book?" he asked at the same time.

Neither spoke for a moment.

"Don't worry about it." Ben kept his voice low so they wouldn't be overheard. "I needed a walk to cool my head."

"That's true enough."

"What about the book? Do you want it?"

"No." She shook her head. "You can hold on to it. We'll look at it later."

She left him on the landing and continued up the stairs to the third floor. When she reached the door to the room, she rummaged for the key. Her fingers landed on something warm and smooth instead. She pulled the aventurine from her pocket and looked at it.

The golden knight stared back at her. She rubbed the glass, but the chess piece held firm.

CHAPTER FOURTEEN

The evening sky glowed with golden light as they strolled to the historic pub, which hugged a curve of cobblestones overlooking a canal. Red trim punctuated the building's whitewashed facade, and a placard over the door declared it "probably the oldest pub in the world."

Birdie, Ben, and Kayla followed Helga and Mrs. Blessing through an entryway past a series of old photographs and into a warm room. Centuries of spilled drinks made the wooden bar shine, while a handful of men in shorts and polo shirts leaned against a massive stone fireplace. They swirled snifters of beer under the watchful eye of the original proprietor, who stared down at them from his faded portrait.

"Our table is out back." Helga waved them through the pub, down a spiral staircase, and into a secluded courtyard. Birdie spotted Uncle Noah and Harry sitting at the end of a long, high-top table near a horseshoe pit.

"Well, there you are now," Harry said, rising as they neared the table. Uncle Noah half-stood, although it seemed like he wasn't sure why. At least he appeared to be in better spirits.

Birdie, Ben, and Kayla arranged themselves on tall stools at the opposite end of the table from the adults, as Ben avoided his uncle's gaze.

"How was the walk?" Harry asked after the women sat down.

"Good." Mrs. Blessing settled onto a stool across from Ben's uncle. "The later it gets, the fewer people to wade through."

"That's the benefit of sleeping over, isn't it?" Helga adjusted her generous frame on the stool beside her husband. "The mornings and evenings are ours to explore without the day-trippers around."

"You know, that's what the guidebook says..." Mrs. Blessing began.

Kayla sighed, pulled out her phone, and began swiping.

Birdie leaned closer to Ben. "What did you do with the book?"

"Brought it." He patted the enlarged pocket of his cargo shorts. "Thought we might get a chance to look at it."

Birdie waited until the waiter took their drink order and the adults resumed their conversation before she continued. "Okay. Let's see it."

He tugged the book from his pocket and held it below the table. He checked to make sure no one was watching, then passed it to her. She glanced up to find her mom absorbed in Helga's description of a tour group and their selfie-sticks, and, curiously, Uncle Noah studying her mom instead of listening to Helga.

"Are you going to open it?"

Birdie turned her attention back to the book in her lap. "Right." She unfolded the thick paper wrapping to reveal the golden knight once again. She pulled the aventurine from her pocket and held it next to the cover.

"Identical," Ben said.

Birdie nodded. "Should I open it?"

"If you don't, I will," Kayla said without looking up from her phone. "What's the big secret, anyway?"

Birdie slipped the glass back into her pocket. "No secret."

The waiter returned with their drinks and jotted the food order on a small tablet, beginning with Helga and working his way around the table. As he departed, Uncle Noah tapped the table once and stood.

"Maria, can I talk to you for a minute?" He gestured toward the spiral stairs that led up to the pub. Birdie's mom nodded, and they excused themselves.

Harry waved them away good-naturedly and then winked at Ben.

"What was that?" Birdie said under her breath.

"No clue," Ben said between his teeth as he nodded and smiled at Harry.

Helga pulled her Marty McEntire book from her bag and nudged her husband.

"Hmmm? What? Oh, yes." He lifted his snowy eyebrows at her. "Yes, yes. We should plan for tomorrow."

"Things just keep getting weirder around here," Birdie said, running a hand across the cover of the book.

"You're telling me. Go ahead and open it before they come back."

She tugged on the rawhide string that kept the book closed. It gave way with a small puff of dust and leather. Birdie glanced at Ben, who nodded toward the knight. She lifted the heavy cover, careful of the binding and the soft pages beneath.

"It's really old," Ben said.

"Yes, but..." She scrutinized it.

"What is it?"

"I don't know. It's strange. It looks ancient, but it feels new."

"What do you mean?"

"Well, feel the leather cover." She held it out so he could touch it. "It's soft and new, but I've never seen a book bound like this before. Have you? And the pages..." She flipped through them tenderly. "They're soft, not brittle like I expected them to be. I figured they'd crumble when I touched them, but they didn't. And the ink is vibrant, too, not faded or running with age."

"I bet it's a reproduction," Kayla said, still without looking up. "There's a bookstore near t'Bruges Huis that has all kinds of new books that are reproductions of old ones. We went there the other day and my grandparents bought one about the ancient city of Troy or something." She shrugged. "It's a tourist thing."

Ben and Birdie exchanged glances.

"Is there a title?" he asked.

Birdie turned past the first blank page.

"*The Game and Playe of the Chesse.*" She had to decipher the peculiar script she found there. "It's an instruction manual."

"In really old script" – he ran a finger over the title –

"that's almost impossible to read."

"Almost, but we should be able to make out some of it."

"At least it's in English," Kayla said. "Could be French or Dutch and then you'd really be up the creek."

"Okay, so why did that boy have the book, and why was that woman chasing him?"

"Stole it," Ben said, sitting back on his stool. He laced his long fingers behind his head and leaned against a wall of ivy-covered bricks behind him. "I bet you a hundred bucks he stole it from that store Kayla's talking about and that nun figured it out and was trying to get it back."

Birdie had to admit it made sense. "Unless…"

Ben raised his eyebrows at her.

"Unless," she continued, "he is trying to learn to play chess."

"From an ancient instruction manual that you can barely read?"

She twisted her lips, searching for an alternative theory. She drew a blank.

"Okay, so now we have stolen property." She closed the book and slid it back to Ben. "Great."

"I hear the prisons here aren't so bad," Kayla said. "Besides, they'd stick you two in juvie, anyway."

"I guess we should take it back to the bookstore," Birdie said, ignoring Kayla. "And tell the owner what happened."

"Hold on now." Ben sat forward and leaned an elbow on the wooden table. His shaggy bangs fell across his eyes and he swept them out of the way. "We don't know what happened, do we? We've got a theory, but—"

"Well, we could at least go to the store and check if they

carry this book." Birdie turned on her stool. "Kayla, how far is the bookstore from the bed-and-breakfast?"

"A few blocks. Not far at all. It's by the gelato shop." She pointed over her shoulder in the general direction of the store. As she did, Birdie's mom and Ben's uncle emerged from the pub and came down the stairs. They crossed the garden to reclaim their seats at the table.

Birdie tried to catch her mom's eye, but Helga had already caught her attention.

Uncle Noah picked up his glass of beer and took a drink.

"So now, tell me about that beer you're drinking," Harry said.

The four adults at the end of the table reminded Birdie of a painting. Their faces were animated in the fading sun, framed by the brick wall crawling with ivy and brightly colored blooms. She took a mental picture and closed her eyes to lock the details into her memory.

"We can see," Ben said as he wrapped the book in its paper cover and put it back in his pocket.

"What?"

"The bookstore? We can ask if we can go. But I'm not sure Uncle Noah will let me out of his sight tomorrow. I've never seen him as hot as he was this afternoon."

"Ask him tonight while he's drunk," Kayla offered, still glued to her screen. "They usually say yes when they're drunk."

Birdie considered Kayla's suggestion. She decided she was glad she didn't know if it was true.

Ben laughed, but there was no humor in it. "You don't know my uncle. He doesn't get drunk. I know he talks a big game about beer and he tries a lot of different types, but he goes for small samples and doesn't really drink that much."

Birdie looked at Uncle Noah's glass. It was a quarter the size of Harry's.

"See what I mean? It's a sample. He'll try one or two more and then call it a night. He's trying to learn about beer, not get annihilated by it."

"Are they free?" Kayla sized up Uncle Noah's glass.

"What? The samples? Sometimes, but I think he normally pays something. Sometimes he can't get the sample size, like when we were at the brewery. He had to take a big beer there, so he just didn't drink it all. Apparently, there are laws here that you can only serve beer in a glass with the brewery or the brand stamped on it. There are all different shapes and sizes of glasses depending on the type of beer, and not every company provides sample sizes."

Kayla nodded, clearly impressed by Ben's knowledge.

"We should ask him about the bookstore when my mom's around," Birdie said, bringing the subject back to the matter at hand. "That might make a difference."

"Worth a shot."

Birdie sipped her soda and waited for the dinner to arrive. She didn't realize how hungry she was until the waiter placed the steaming plate of spaghetti with meat sauce in front of her. A basket of fresh bread and butter appeared a few seconds later.

"How is it?" her mom called from the other end of the table.

"Awesome." Birdie meant it, even if she was beginning to wonder if she'd eat spaghetti every night.

Mrs. Blessing nodded and dug into her soup and toasted sandwich.

Dessert followed dinner as the daylight faded.

"It's got to be late." Birdie glanced at the sky.

"I wonder how much longer they're going to want to stay," Ben said.

"Hey, do you guys mind if we walk back to the B and B?" Kayla called up the table.

The adults exchanged glances.

"I'd prefer if you stayed here and walked back with us," Mrs. Blessing said. "It's getting late."

Kayla's grandparents nodded in agreement.

She scowled and lost herself in her phone again.

Ben and Birdie settled back onto their stools.

At least they had a plan.

An hour later, the sun's last orange ribbon slipped across the canal into moonlit darkness as Ben and Birdie trailed the others back to the bed-and-breakfast. They'd kept themselves occupied at the pub, playing bowles in the horseshoe pit, which the waiter explained was a game where each player rolled heavy stone wheels toward a stake in the ground to see who could get them closest. Birdie and Ben had hit both the stake and several of the tables around the pit.

Deep shadows stretched across the narrow lane, broken only by occasional puddles of light from the lantern-like street lamps. Birdie shoved her hands in her jacket pockets. She cupped the aventurine in her fingers and felt it grow warm.

A few blocks away, church bells rang out a hymn to close the day.

They were nearly at t'Bruges Huis when she saw him.

"Ben," she whispered, but he didn't hear her over the chimes.

She squinted to make out the figure in the dark.

She pushed on Ben's arm. "Do you see him?"

Ben slowed and followed Birdie's gaze down the alley to the canal wall they'd sat on that afternoon. Halfway down the block, a sandy-haired, barefooted boy in pants that were too wide and long, sat with his legs dangling over the edge of the wall. A blanket of fog hugged the water behind him, casting a shimmering glow that lit the night.

They stopped.

The others continued on, deep in conversation.

"It's him," she breathed.

"I see him," Ben said. He allowed a quick glance at the grown-ups. "They'll hear me if I call to him."

Birdie nodded in agreement.

"What should we do?"

She lifted her hand to wave. As she did, the boy jumped from the wall and started jogging toward them.

"He's coming." She drew in her breath. "I can't believe it. He's coming."

"I can take him," Ben said, adjusting his stance.

Birdie placed a hand on his clenched fist and lowered it. "Of course you can. He's half your size. Let's hope that won't be necessary."

He relaxed a little, and she dropped her hand. The boy was less than three houses away.

"Ben!" Uncle Noah barked. Ben jumped and reformed his gangly fight stance, only this time pointed up the cobblestone lane toward his uncle.

Birdie turned just in time to catch her mother shush Uncle Noah. She recognized the action, Jonah having been on the receiving end of it so many times.

Birdie held up her index finger. "Just a sec," she whisper-yelled back.

"Now," Uncle Noah bellowed, ignoring her mom.

Ben tensed beside her.

"It's okay," she said. "Go."

"What about you?"

Birdie turned back to the alley. "I'll talk to…"

But the boy was no longer moving toward them. He was running the other way.

"Wait!" She cried, no longer caring who heard her.

But the boy didn't wait, and a moment later he reached a curve along the wall and faded out of sight.

"Let's go," Ben said. "Son of a…" He kicked at the cobblestones and started walking.

She watched the spot where the boy had disappeared for a moment longer and then fell into step beside Ben.

"Don't get into it with your uncle," she said. "Please. I'm too tired to listen to it and if you tick him off, he won't let you come to the bookstore with me tomorrow."

He shot her a disapproving look and then softened. "Yeah, whatever. I don't need a fight either."

When the adults saw them on their way, they resumed their pace toward the bed-and-breakfast. Kayla loitered between the two groups, as if she were too cool for the grown-ups and too old for Ben and Birdie.

"We should follow him." Ben was staring at his uncle's back several yards in front of them.

"What? We already are."

"No, not Uncle Noah. That kid. We should sneak out tonight and figure out where he ran off to."

"No way," Birdie said.

"Why not?"

"What if we get caught?"

"I won't be in any worse trouble than I am now."

"But I will be. Besides, we don't know where he went."

Ben shrugged. "He probably went home."

"Maybe," she said. "Hopefully."

"Hey." He paused as if he were going to turn back. "Do you think you could try to find his house again?"

"Right now?"

"No. Tomorrow. When we go to the bookstore."

"If you can go."

"Yes, if I can go."

She thought about it. "I don't know. I got all turned around this afternoon when we tried. We'd need to go back to where my mom and I were on that canal cruise. The streets and the houses look so much alike it's hard to tell them apart. This town is so confusing."

Uncle Noah checked to make sure they were still following them.

"Come on." She resumed her pace. "Things always look brighter in the morning."

CHAPTER FIFTEEN

"So, what do you know about chess?" Ben asked his uncle the next morning at breakfast. He'd made his first appearance at Mrs. Devon's table since Birdie and her mom arrived.

"The basics. It's a strategy game." Uncle Noah reached across the table to retrieve a tiny jar of yogurt and two pieces of toast from the tray in the center of the table. "Complicated, but once they understand how to play, people seem to enjoy it."

"Do you know how to play?"

"I learned in fifth grade, so let's just say I'd be a little rusty. It's a game where every piece can make its own moves. Some can only move forward, some only sideways, some diagonally. You have to play a lot to get the hang of it." He took a generous bite of toast and chewed it before addressing Birdie's mom. "What about you? Do you know how to play?"

"I do," she said.

"Really?" Birdie asked.

"Really."

Birdie drew a blank at first, but then an image fought its way to her mind as if it were floating to her from a deep sleep. She remembered the weathered wooden chessboard on the sprawling front porch of a lake house in New York. How long had it been? Five years? Yes. It had been the summer of fourth grade.

Everything had been so different then.

They'd spent a lot of weekends away before everything changed, most of them tied to Jonah's baseball tournaments. They'd been tossing a ball back and forth at the water's edge while their parents played chess, laughing and drinking wine that was so clear the sun sparkled through the goblets.

Jonah had been rough with the hard ball, throwing it to her like she was one of his teammates. She'd pretended it was fine, but the palms of her hands stung at the memory.

Then, to her horror, her eyes began to sting.

"You okay, Birdie?" Uncle Noah paused part way through explaining the moves the queen could make.

She swallowed as she pushed the memory away and willed the tears not to fall. "Yep, I'm good. I just forgot that my mom knew how to play, that's all."

"Do you know the moves the knight can make?" Ben asked, as if he hadn't heard his uncle's question.

"Hmmm," Mrs. Blessing said, leaning forward to study Birdie before turning her attention to Ben. "I'd almost need a board to show you. The knight moves sort of diagonally, but it has to land on a different vertical or horizontal line than it's already on. Here. Look."

"It's also the only piece that can leap over other pieces,"

Uncle Noah said as Mrs. Blessing tried to demonstrate the proper movement using yogurt jars and glasses of juice.

Mrs. Devon entered through the swinging door and raised her eyebrows at the makeshift game board.

"Oh, this is no good," Mrs. Blessing said, returning each item to its proper place.

"I'm sure we'll come across a chess board somewhere," Uncle Noah said. "I'll show you then."

Her mom leaned in close as Uncle Noah talked to Ben. "It's okay," she said softly before straightening again. "So today," she continued at her normal volume, "we're going to visit the Jerusalem Chapel and the Lace Museum. That shouldn't take long if we get there before the crowds. Then I want to go back to Burg Square to do some final sketching, and then, if there's time, take one more stroll to make sure we didn't miss anything fabulous before we leave for Germany tomorrow."

"Wait, we're leaving tomorrow?" Birdie asked, the chessboard forgotten.

"That's the plan. I think we've seen about everything here, haven't we? We hit all the highlights in the Marty McEntire book for sure."

Birdie opened her mouth but words failed her.

"Except for the bookstore," Ben said.

Birdie glanced at him hopefully.

"No, I don't think Marty mentioned a specific bookstore," her mom said, then lifted her eyes to the ceiling. "Well, I take that back. Maybe he did. I kind of remember seeing a list of places that sell his guidebooks."

"I'm not sure, ma'am. But Kayla told us there is this cool

bookstore in town."

"This from the kid who turned in his book report a month late." Uncle Noah sat back in his chair and draped a long arm across the empty one next to him.

Ben ignored him. "We were talking about it at dinner last night. We were kind of hoping to go see it."

Mrs. Blessing considered them for a moment.

"Well," she said, drawing her attention back to Ben's uncle, "what are you two up to today?"

"I'm picking up a rental car in" — he pressed the button on his phone to see the time — "thirty minutes. Then we're heading out to the Westvleteren Abbey."

"What's at the abbey?" Mrs. Blessing asked.

Uncle Noah gave her a withering look. "It's only considered to be the place where the very best beer in the world is brewed."

"Oh. Of course it is. And it's housed in an old abbey?"

"Monks make the beer," he said. "There are quite a few monastery beers brewed in Belgium and in other places across Europe. It's an old tradition that makes them money."

"And I bet we're fixing to see them all," Ben said under his breath.

"Most of them," Uncle Noah said cheerfully, tipping his glass of orange juice at Ben in a toast. "But Westvleteren is the toughest to get into. They don't want people disturbing the monks."

"Do I have to go?" Ben asked.

"What else will you do? Besides, you'll get to see some of the countryside and learn how the monks brew the beer. It's only about an hour away."

Ben slumped in his chair.

"Well, if you don't mind tombs and lace, you're welcome to explore the town with Birdie and me today. We could make a point of stopping at that bookstore," Mrs. Blessing said. "With your uncle's permission, of course."

"Oh, of course." The corner of Uncle Noah's mouth twitched as he tried not to smile.

"Can I?"

Birdie held her breath.

It was a moment before Uncle Noah responded. He locked eyes with Mrs. Blessing. "Sure, Ben. You can stay here with Birdie. As long as Mrs. Blessing is sure she doesn't mind."

"Well, that's great," Birdie's mom said, plucking the napkin from her lap and wiping her mouth to hide her own smile. "We'd love the extra company. When do you expect to be back?"

"With the tour and the drive, not until about six tonight."

"Very good. We'll be sure to be back by then so we can deliver Ben safely into your care."

Ben coughed as his orange juice went down the wrong pipe. Birdie slapped him hard on the back and he stopped sputtering.

"Problem?" Uncle Noah asked him.

Ben swallowed. "No, sir."

"Then thank Mrs. Blessing for offering to let you hang out with them today."

"Thank you, Mrs. Blessing."

"You're welcome, Ben."

The rest of the breakfast passed quickly. Uncle Noah finished his meal, handed Ben money for lunch, and then excused himself to catch the taxi Mrs. Devon had arranged for him to pick up the rental car. Ben waited in the sitting room while Birdie and her mom went upstairs to get their things. Ten minutes later, they were standing beneath the brick steeple of the Jerusalem Chapel. A giant green orb capped the point, which was flanked by a spire on each side. One spire was topped by a golden sun, the other by a golden moon.

"There's nobody here." Birdie turned in a circle and peered down each of the curved lanes around them.

"Perfect," her mom said, pulling out her sketchbook.

They followed her under a brick archway and into a formal garden, where they found a ticket booth and entrances to a small museum, a coffee shop, and the chapel. Ben handed Mrs. Blessing a few heavy coins, and she bought three tickets.

They visited the garden and museum first, then headed to the chapel. It was much smaller than the Church of Our Lady, and Ben had to fold himself nearly in half to get through the low-slung door leading into the sanctuary. Even Birdie had to duck.

Inside, the sun shone through windows that rose all the way to the top of the steeple. Woodcarvings and paintings of the Madonna and Child adorned the brick walls. A black marble tomb rose from the middle of the floor, with a man and woman sculpted onto its surface. The woman wore a traditional Dutch dress and hat that looked like a witch costume, and a dog lay under her feet. The man wore armor; his pointed boots rested atop a carved lion.

A stone altar stood beyond the tomb. It was carved as if it were an excavation site, with bones, skulls, lanterns, rope, and tools protruding from its surface. Candles flickered before it.

"Wicked," Ben whispered, as they followed Birdie's mom through a hidden passageway behind the altar and down a short set of stairs into another chamber.

At the far end, a wrought-iron gate stood open.

The opening for the gate was even shorter than the door had been, and Birdie ducked low to make her way through it. Inside, behind an ornate metal grate, a lifelike sculpture of a nearly naked Jesus lay on a slab, staring toward heaven from beneath his crown of thorns.

"What is this place?" Birdie asked, suddenly overcome with the thought that the sculpture might open its eyes and start talking to them, or worse, reach through the metal grate that surrounded it and grab her ankle. She took a step back and bumped into the brick wall.

"It's a replica of a church in Jerusalem that was built over Christ's tomb," her mom said.

"Why?" Birdie asked as Ben bent down low to check out the savior's face.

Mrs. Blessing tugged her guidebook from her bag and turned to a dog-eared page near the front. She held it near the candle so she could see the text. "This says that the man who built it was very faithful and traveled to Jerusalem in the 1400s when few people would have done such a thing." She closed the book. "So he built it to show his devotion to God."

"Oh."

"Good thing he did too," Ben said, standing up as far as he could, which wasn't very far. "The original one was destroyed."

"How do you know that?" Birdie asked. For a split second, she wondered if the sculpture had whispered it to him, but she shook the thought away.

"Saw it in the Marty McEntire book," he said, gesturing at the one in Mrs. Blessing's hands.

Birdie raised her eyebrows at him.

"What?" He spread his hands wide. "Do you have any idea how many breweries we've been to? I needed something to do to keep from going crazy."

"So you read Marty McEntire books?"

He shrugged. "It was that or the book about all the breweries."

"What about the book for your report?" Birdie asked.

"Very funny," Ben said.

"Okay." Birdie's mom checked her watch. "Why don't you two go into the coffee shop and have some hot chocolate? I just have a few more things to sketch in here. I won't be long. It looked like there were some comfy couches in there."

She didn't have to tell them twice.

Thirty minutes later, with two stomachs full of cocoa and one sketchbook full of drawings, they made the short walk to the lace museum. They started at the gift shop and ticket desk, which sat on the ground floor of a large, walled-off building, which was surrounded by a lush garden like the church had been.

"I would love to learn how to make this lace," Mrs. Blessing said, holding a piece up and examining its intricate design in the sunlight that came through a tall casement window.

"There's a class," Birdie said.

"There is?"

She pointed to a bulletin board that hung nearby.

Her mom studied the flyer that listed the class information, then shook her head.

"I don't think that's going to work." She glanced at the time. "The class starts in about five minutes, but it lasts all afternoon. We'd never make it to the bookstore and we haven't had lunch, not that I'm starving after Mrs. Devon's breakfast, but—"

"You could stay, Mom, and take the class, and Ben and I could go to the bookstore and then stop somewhere for lunch."

"Oh, I don't know." She glanced around the shop before settling her gaze on Ben. "What would your uncle say?"

"I don't think he'd mind, do you, Ben? It's okay with me, anyway," Birdie said. "Really. I'd much rather go to that bookstore than learn to make lace."

Mrs. Blessing looked at Ben. "What about you?"

He held up his long, crooked fingers. "Ma'am, I don't think these hands were built for making lace."

She laughed. "Okay then. I'll stay and take the class and you two can go to the bookstore and get some lunch. Take your time because I won't be done until after five. You can meet me back at the bed-and-breakfast."

She dug into her pocket and handed Birdie some money and her wrinkled map. "Don't be late. And stay together. Don't talk to strangers."

"Mom—"

"And be careful. Watch where you're going. Do you know where you're going? The drivers—"

"Are maniacs. I know, Mom."

"Yes, of course you do. But still—"

"We'll be careful, and I think we can find our way. Kayla said the bookstore isn't far from the bed-and-breakfast."

"Okay. If you're sure." She gave Birdie a quick hug and headed toward the registration desk. She was almost there when she turned around.

"Oh, and have fun," she said, a smile lighting her face.

"Now we can try to find the boy's house," Ben said as soon as they were outside and making their way down the cobblestone lane that curved around the Jerusalem Chapel. "You said you thought you could find it if we went back to the place where you and your mom went on the canal cruise."

"Did you bring the book?"

Ben patted his pocket.

"We can try. But I'm not making any promises."

They made their way to t'Bruges Huis and then retraced the route she and her mom took to the dock the day before. There were entrances for canal cruises all over town, and Birdie wasn't sure she'd find the right one unless they went all the way back to the beginning.

The lanes grew more and more crowded as they wound

their way to the entrance.

"We're almost there," she said.

Ben looked around as if he expected to see the boy run past.

They climbed to the center of the bridge, then stepped to the side to allow the other tourists to pass. The canal flowed beneath them, broken only by the rumble of the tourist boats.

"There." Birdie pointed at one as it glided out from beneath the bridge. "That's the way we went too. Do you see the spot with the small dock? The canal curves there and you can't see what's around the bend."

Ben nodded.

"That's where the buildings start again. That's where I saw him go into a house."

They crossed onto the narrow lane that bordered the canal and followed it until they reached the bend. As Birdie predicted, the green space gave way to tall houses.

"They all look so similar," she said, shaking her head. "It's hard to say which one it was."

They continued for a short distance before Birdie stopped again.

"Wait. Let me think." She sat on the wall next to the canal. Ben stood beside her, one sneakered foot propped up on the stones. She surveyed the houses.

"Only some of them have flowers," she said.

Ben cocked his head and spread his hands apart.

Birdie studied the flowers that tumbled from the window boxes.

"Wait, that's it! That's the one." She pointed to a brick

house that rose three stories from the canal. She considered the facade. "But the flowers in the window boxes are a different color. They were purple and red yesterday. I thought it was such an odd color combination when I saw him go in."

"I'm not seeing any purple flowers, Birdie."

"They're not purple now. They're pink and yellow. Someone must have changed them out. But I recognize the coats of arms painted on the window boxes. Come on, let's go."

"But—"

"Just trust me."

You'll find flowers at every turn throughout Europe, and Bruges is no exception. Homeowners and businesses take pride in the colorful displays that grace window boxes and planters no matter what time of year you visit. During the winter holidays, watch for evergreens to take the place of the pansies, petunias, and begonias that brighten the spring and summer months.

—*Marty McEntire,* Europe for Americans Travel Guide

CHAPTER SIXTEEN

They stepped onto the stoop of the red brick house.

"We're doing this?" Ben asked.

"Do you want to find him or not?" Birdie tugged on a long iron rod hanging near the arched door, then pulled harder when nothing happened.

A heavy bell clanged inside.

"Here, hold this." He extracted the book from his pocket.

They waited, but no one came.

"Looks like nobody's home," she said.

Ben nodded toward the rod, and she reached to pull it again but stopped when she heard movement behind the door. Ten seconds later, a metal lock scraped, and the door eased open little more than a crack.

A tiny woman with gray-and-white curls peered through the opening. Her eyebrows were the same twist of color, and heavy lids hooded her pale blue eyes.

She stared at them but didn't speak.

Birdie's mouth went dry.

"*Pardon*, ma'am," Ben said in creaky Dutch. "*Specht Engels?*"

The woman tilted her head sharply to inspect Ben, then nodded.

"We are… we found this book," he said, switching to English. He pointed to the bound volume in Birdie's hands. She loosened her grip on the package and peeled back the paper, revealing the golden knight on the cover. "We thought it might belong to the boy who lives here."

The old woman narrowed her eyes at Ben. "No boys live here," she said, her voice a light soprano that was startling in contrast to her suspicious glare.

"But… oh, but are you sure? I saw him the other day." Birdie stepped forward. "He came in through the front door."

"You did? Hmmm. I can assure you no boys live in my house. I am sorry, my dear, but you are mistaken." She stared hard at Birdie. "There are no children here."

"But…" She hesitated as the woman's eyes grew wide. "I could have sworn… he was dressed like one of the historical reenactors. And there was a little girl, too, in the window upstairs."

The woman chuckled and shook her head, causing her hair to look like a gray and white feather duster picked up in the breeze.

"You'll see no reenactors in the summer, I'm afraid. Not anymore. It's too hot these days for all that wool. I am sorry, but you have the wrong house. No children have lived here since my daughters were young."

"We're sorry to have disturbed you, ma'am." Ben took a

half step back and tapped Birdie's elbow.

"No problem at all." The woman considered him for a moment, then smiled suddenly, revealing off-colored teeth. "You are American?"

"Yes," he said.

"We were on the brewery roof," Birdie said, "and I thought I saw the boy who lives here at the park. Then we found this book and… I'm really sor—"

"I said it is no problem." The woman lowered her eyelids in a way that told Birdie not to apologize again. "But since you rang my bell, would you care to come off that stoop and join me for tea?"

She pulled the heavy door open expectantly.

"Thank you, ma'am, but…"

Birdie kicked Ben's sneaker. "Yes, thank you," she said. "That would be lovely."

"This way."

They crossed the threshold into a vestibule, and the woman locked the solid wooden door behind them. She shuffled across the small space and opened a second, taller door that featured two stained-glass panels that caught the light from the foyer beyond. On the top, a yellow lion curled around a green tree, and on the bottom, a white bear stood on its hind legs.

She steadied herself against an ancient accent table as she led them through the foyer and into a parlor that was similar to the sitting room at t'Bruges Huis. She gestured to two well-worn chairs and a dusky blue love seat as she reached for the silver tray on the coffee table. "Please sit down. I will heat the water."

Ben met Birdie's eyes as they settled into the chairs.

"Why did you say yes?" he whispered after the door to the kitchen closed.

Birdie leaned in. "Those kids were here. I'm sure of it."

"Well, they're not here now."

"I know that, but maybe we can learn something useful. Maybe we should show her what's in the book."

He sat back and crossed his ankle over his knee. "Okay. But I think we're wasting our time."

Birdie didn't bother to argue with him. She shifted in her chair to examine the fireplace instead. Flowers, cherubs, fairies, and vines adorned a carved mantle, where a yellowed photograph of a young couple in their wedding clothes sat next to a blue-and-gold curio box. An elegantly curved mirror reflected the room back to them, capturing the molding that outlined the painted ceiling. Their reflections were faded and out of time in the aged glass.

Beneath their sneakers was a rug that was more like a tapestry than a carpet, with round storybook vignettes. One section showed a mother and children in a field, another a father in black clothing, and a third, angels in heaven welcoming them all. There were other scenes, too, but the furniture covered them.

Birdie picked up her feet and examined the soles of her sneakers. The last thing she wanted was to drag dirt onto the rug. She always took her shoes off at home. She hadn't thought of doing it here. Until now.

"Here we go." The woman shuffled into the room. "Fresh and hot."

She set the tray on the coffee table and placed a dainty

119

cup and saucer in front of each of them.

"Now," she said as she poured the steaming brown liquid into their cups, "how do you take your tea?"

"With milk and sugar," Birdie said, thinking of the only other time she'd had tea.

"And you, young man?"

"Same way, please, ma'am."

"Aha." She fixed the tea for them without another question.

Birdie didn't know the proper way to take tea, and she would have bet money this was the first time Ben was trying it. The teacup looked ridiculous in front of him, like he was playing tea party with a bunch of dolls.

But this was no party.

She closed her eyes for longer than a blink and steadied herself.

When she opened them, she reconsidered the woman preparing their tea. She wore bright coral slacks and a coordinating sweater, with a lovely pendant necklace falling on her speckled chest.

Birdie silently admonished herself for her first impression of the woman, which had been so dark and heavy. Now, in the parlor, fresh tea steaming in front of them, the bright light streaming through the lace window sheers, she looked like a nice old lady.

"So tell me, what is it that brings you to Bruges, all the way across the ocean?" she asked as she settled onto the love seat.

"I came with my mom. She's a designer. She's developing a new medieval-themed line of clothing and home accessories and wanted to visit different places in Europe for ideas."

"I see. And this great designer, she is your mother too?"

"Oh, no, ma'am." Ben's cup tittered against the saucer as he spoke.

"You are not brother and sister, then?"

Birdie gulped, and Ben answered. "No, ma'am. We just met at the bed-and-breakfast."

"Oh, I see. Fast friends then? Which bed-and-breakfast might that be?"

"t'Bruges Huis," he said. "A woman named Mrs. Devon owns it."

"Certainly. I know Mrs. Devon well. She is the niece of my good friend Alma, God rest her soul. Alma died last year. Did you know?"

They looked at her blankly.

"No, no, of course you didn't. Sad story, really. I'm not sure they ever found the taxi driver who hit her. She was crossing Steenstraat with a bag of apricots from the Wednesday market and then, well, you know the rest, I suppose."

The woman took a long sip of the steaming tea, leaving a bright slash of coral lipstick on the rim of the cup.

Birdie didn't dare to look at Ben.

"And what have you done so far in our fair city?"

"A lot." Birdie listed the sites she'd visited with her mom. "And we went to the brewery, too, and took a bike ride to the windmills."

"Yes, well, we are known for our great brewery. Did you know it is the oldest in the area?"

"Yes," Birdie said. "Our tour guide told us all about it."

"Oh, good. Who was your guide?"

"Elsa."

"Oh, you were lucky then. She is the best one, in English anyway. My husband always requested her for his tour groups, God rest his soul. Not that we had many Americans then. No, not many at all. A few. Mostly the English speakers came from Great Britain, although sometimes the Germans preferred the tour in English if they wanted to practice the language. There were the Chinese tourists too. Sometimes they took the English tour, but never as part of my husband's groups. They brought their own tour guides from China."

She smiled at them over her cup and took another sip. She gripped the cup with gnarled fingers on both hands. Birdie noticed three rings on each hand, each one with a different brightly colored stone.

"And what about you, young man? You are awfully quiet. What brings you to Bruges?"

"My uncle brews his own beer at home, and he's thinking about starting a brewery. We're here so he can try different types across Europe."

"Hmmm. Across Europe? Well, Belgium has the best beer in all of Europe, he will find. Not that I partake much myself. I prefer tea."

"That's what he said, too, about Belgium, I mean. But he feels the need to try beer in several countries just to be sure."

The woman chuckled. "Yes, yes, of course he does. If you believe what you read in the newspaper, though, it is the United States that has the best breweries. Loads of little ones springing up all over the place."

"That's what my uncle wants to open," Ben said. "A little

one. They call them craft breweries."

"Yes, yes, that is right. You are absolutely correct, young man."

She studied them a moment.

"And what are your names?"

"I'm Ben."

"Birdie."

"Ah, suitable names, to be sure. I am Mrs. Olinda Winggen."

Although they may seem unapproachable, don't be afraid to ask a local for advice. Learn a few words in their language and chances are they'll be more than willing to give you the inside scoop on their favorite places.

—*Marty McEntire,* Europe for Americans Travel Guide

CHAPTER SEVENTEEN

"Mrs. Winggen, when we were on the porch, you said you've lived here since you were a little girl," Birdie said.

"Indeed, I have. I've lived here my whole life. First with my parents, then with my husband, Alan, before he passed, God rest his soul." She pronounced her husband's name *uh-lawn*.

"Is that the two of you?" Birdie pointed to the photo on the mantel.

"Yes, dear. Many years ago." She twisted her lips, thinking hard. "Let's see. We would have been married sixty-two years now, if he were still alive."

Birdie thought about the photograph of her mom in a white gown, her arm wrapped warmly around her father in his black tuxedo, smiling like Mr. and Mrs. Winggen. It was too sad to consider how short their marriage had been.

"Your house is awesome. Has your family always owned it?" Ben asked, turning away from the mantel.

"Oh, not always, no." She swished the silly idea away with her bejeweled fingers. "But we've had it for, oh, let me see." She glanced at the ceiling as if it held a clue. "Five hundred years, I suppose."

Ben and Birdie exchanged glances.

"Before that, it belonged to a merchant who traveled to Venice from time to time. He was quite wealthy and the leader of one of the guilds. The guildsmen were in charge of everything back then, as you know, I'm sure. He built and staffed this house for his wife and family. We were the two big places then, Venice and Bruges."

"Five hundred years?" Birdie said.

Mrs. Winggen sipped her tea. "Ah, yes. Five hundred, give or take a few. My family took charge of the house after the merchant and his wife succumbed to the plague. So sad. She was French. His wife, I mean."

"French?" Ben asked.

"Yes, we mixed things up back then with the French and the English. But still we kept our Dutch heritage in Bruges. There were many languages back then. There still are, I suppose. It's one reason we get so many tourists. But that is just my opinion."

"You speak English so well," Ben said.

"I suppose I do. I helped my husband in his business, God rest his soul."

Birdie sipped her tea as she listened to Mrs. Winggen. It was hot and bitter on the tip of her tongue, despite the sugar and cream. It was nothing like the tea she had before, which tasted strongly of cinnamon and was a million times sweeter. But that tea had been at the elementary school, where they dressed up and pretended to be on the *Titanic*. Her teacher must have sweetened it up so they'd drink it.

"Do you like the tea, dear?" Mrs. Winggen set her cup on its saucer. "Do you need another lump of sugar?"

Birdie nodded and Mrs. Winggen dropped a cube of tan-colored sugar the size of a Monopoly die into her dainty cup. She gestured to Ben with the sugar grabber.

"And you, young man?"

"Three more."

"Very good."

"Thank you." Birdie stirred the dissolving cube in her tea.

"So, tell me about this book you found." Mrs. Winggen poured herself another cup. "You said you thought it belonged to a boy who lived here? Yes, too bad. The last time a boy lived here, it was my father, and before that, his father. It has been, oh, I would say, at least a hundred years since anyone you could consider a boy lived here."

"Were you an only child?" Ben asked.

"I had a sister, a few years older than me, but she passed, God rest her soul. I have two daughters of my own, and someday they will live here. Or at least one of them will. They'll need to work that out, I suppose. After five hundred years, the house must stay in the family, don't you agree? Besides, they loved it here when they were girls."

"Where are they now?" Ben asked.

"In Brussels, working, raising their own children. I see them from time to time. Not much work here in Bruges unless you cater to the tourist trade. Alan made a good living on tourism, you understand, bringing groups here. Put the girls on a good path in life. We had fun back then, taking people around. It wasn't like today, no. Now everyone with a credit card and a Marty McEntire book comes traipsing through. Back then, only those with real money vacationed in a forgotten city like Bruges."

"Why do you call it that? Forgotten?" Birdie asked.

"Because it was, you see." She leaned back against the cushions. "After the port silted up, the merchant ships stopped coming. People left to find work, or they died from the plague. For hundreds of years, it was as if Bruges didn't exist at all. But then, in the 1800s, the artists and painters – they were the Romantics you know – they discovered our charms and riches and we became a stop on the grand tour that aristocrats took when they came of age."

She stared into her teacup. "My daughters will probably retire here, if I had to imagine. It is a lovely place to live, out of the bustle of the big city, as long as we can keep the tourists in check."

They sat quietly for a moment. Birdie sipped her tea, which was much better with the extra lump.

"Mrs. Winggen," she said, "when your husband ran the tour company, did he ever hear of a special piece of glass from Venice? It's called aventurine."

"Aventurine?" She set her teacup down and eyed Birdie curiously. "A fool's quest if ever there was one. They sell replicas of it in the gift shops around town. Every so often, I see a young person with one. A whole lot of rubbish, if you ask me."

"So you don't believe in the legend?" Ben asked.

"Believe in magic? Of course not. Now don't

misunderstand me, Bruges feels like a magical place, of course, because of its history and beauty, so people think there is more to it than that. But there is not. The only real magic here is in the imaginations of the tourists."

She lifted the kettle from the tray and topped off her cup. "Now, Alan, he believed."

"Your husband?" Ben said.

"Yes. He believed in the legend of the aventurine completely. I think he adored the idea of going back in time for real, not just talking about the past to his tour groups."

"You must miss him," Birdie said.

"Indeed." She sipped her tea, lost in thought. Then she shook her head. "Okay. Enough melancholy. Tell me more about this book you found." She nodded to the leather-bound lump in Birdie's lap.

"We found it under a tree in the park near the Begijnhof," she said. "We think a boy dropped it there when he was running from one of the nuns."

Mrs. Winggen chuckled. "Oh, now, I cannot imagine one of the Benedictine sisters chasing a child through the Minnewater. That's the name of that park, the Minnewater."

"It looked like he was hiding from her." She settled her empty teacup on its saucer on the coffee table.

"Is there any chance it was a boy and girl who live nearby?" Ben asked. "Maybe Birdie got the wrong house."

Birdie was certain this was not the case, but she chose not to correct Ben in front of Mrs. Winggen. Besides, the woman had already made it clear she found their tale far-fetched.

"I'm afraid not. Half of the houses are vacant and for

sale — at silly prices if you ask me — and the others are owned by older people like me or rented out like Mrs. Devon's. No children."

"Oh." Ben looked disappointed.

"What is the book about?" Her blue eyes sparkled as the sun filtered through the window sheers. The pattern of the light reminded Birdie of her mother several blocks away, learning to weave lace by hand. She would kill her if she knew they were in some stranger's house sipping tea.

"Chess," Birdie said. "It's an instruction manual."

Mrs. Winggen gave her an odd look. It was several moments before she spoke, and Birdie began to wonder if she'd heard her.

"Perhaps the book has the boy's name inside the front cover. People do that sometimes, especially with leather-bound books that are expensive or private. They want to make sure the book gets back to them if they lose it."

Birdie glanced at the book in her lap. Her eyes narrowed.

The embossed knight that had been so bright and gold when they stood on the stoop now held only faint hints of color, pale reds and greens, perhaps a touch of what was once yellow. It looked different than it had at the pub.

"Why don't you open it and check," Ben encouraged her.

CHAPTER EIGHTEEN

Birdie tugged at the rawhide that held the book closed. The bow held tight, refusing to break free.

"Is it stuck?" Ben leaned forward. He looked as if he might get up to help.

Birdie grasped the rawhide at a spot closer to the bow and pulled harder. It scratched through the knot and, with a small spray of dust, came undone. The rawhide fell onto her lap, still wrapped snuggly around the back cover. She turned the book over and discovered a series of belt loops securing the thin piece of leather. They hadn't been there the night before.

She lifted the cover, which stuck as if it'd never been cracked before.

The first page was yellowed and blank.

Birdie turned the page and discovered a paragraph handwritten in a careful, elegant script. She stared at it, amazed. She'd have sworn that paragraph wasn't there when they examined the book at the pub the night before.

She couldn't make out the writing.

"Is it his name?" Ben asked.

She held the book out to Mrs. Winggen. "Can you read what this says? I think it's in Dutch."

"Let me look." She pulled a pair of glasses from the pocket of her sweater and slipped them on. She accepted the book from Birdie and held it open about a foot from her face, squinting at the curlicue script through the colorful plastic frames.

"No, dear, I don't think this is Dutch. It may be... I don't know, could it be Celtic? Celtic, yes, that could be it. Which, unfortunately, I do not read."

"That's strange," Ben said. "Why would it be written in Celtic? That seems so unlikely."

"To be here, you mean?" Birdie asked.

"Well, yes, to be here, but to exist at all. I thought the Celtic language was primarily an oral tradition, not something someone would've used in an old printed book. I saw a show about it on TV."

"It's handwritten," Birdie said. "There are handwritten words at the beginning."

"No, there—" Ben began.

"Yes," she cut him off and opened her eyes wide, "there are."

"I can guarantee you the boy who had this is not the owner," Mrs. Winggen said, closing the book and tucking it into her lap with a protective grip. "It's extremely old and few people outside of Ireland know the language anymore. Even they are doing all they can to preserve it."

Birdie opened her hand in silent request.

Mrs. Winggen pulled the book closer. "Would you like me to hold on to it to see if I can find the owners?"

"Thank you for offering," Birdie said with more politeness than she felt. "But we have some ideas about where to look next."

The old woman loosened her hold on the volume and handed it back, looking all the while as if she'd prefer to slip it into the pocket of her coral sweater instead.

Birdie lifted the cover again and studied the script, but it meant nothing to her. The neat handwriting continued on the next page, beginning at the top edge and continuing all the way to the bottom, not wasting any space. She glanced at the next tightly written page, cautious of the brittle paper.

"I could take it back to the Benedictines at the Begijnhof for you," Mrs. Winggen offered. "The caretakers may have some idea where it belongs. Yes, yes, that would be the place it most likely came from, since you found it at the Minnewater."

Birdie thought about the nun chasing the boy. Maybe she was after him for a good reason. Maybe he'd stolen the book from the Begijnhof, not the bookstore.

"Now, now, don't look so glum," Mrs. Winggen said when neither Birdie nor Ben accepted her offer. "I'm sure you'll sort this out. How long will you be in Bruges?"

"One more day." Birdie eyed the knight doubtfully as she wrapped it in the protective paper. "That doesn't give us much time."

"No, it doesn't. But maybe you won't need much time. Time is a funny thing, you know. It expands and contracts to suit itself. Some days seem to last forever and others fly by." She snapped her fingers. "Perhaps tomorrow will be one of those days."

"I hope you're right. Thank you for the tea, Mrs. Winggen. It was very kind of you."

"It was my pleasure. I always love a little company with my afternoon tea. And please bring that to me if you don't find its owner before you leave. I'll see it gets into the proper hands."

They left through the vestibule after another round of goodbyes, during which Mrs. Winggen jotted her phone number on a slip of yellow paper and handed it to Birdie.

"Tuck that inside for safekeeping, so you know how to reach me if you don't finish your quest before you leave Bruges."

They walked along the canal in silence until they reached the bridge.

"Hold up," Ben said when they were halfway across.

"What is it?"

He leaned against the stone wall that served as a railing and stared into the languid water. In the distance, Mrs. Winggen's front door was shut tight once again. If it weren't for the pink and yellow flowers tumbling from the window boxes, it would appear as if no one lived there at all.

"The book changed," he said.

"I know."

"What do you think is going on?"

Birdie didn't respond.

Ben turned to face her.

"I have no idea," she said. "None of this makes any sense at all. It's ancient now, like it aged five hundred years in five minutes."

"Can I see it?"

She sat on the wall and handed him the package. He unwrapped it, opened the cover with extreme care, and tenderly turned the page.

The beautiful script was still there, taunting them with its curlicues and long elegant swoops, woven into letters and words she didn't understand.

"A traveler's journal," Ben said.

"Maybe. But we can't read it to be sure. Mrs. Winggen said it was in Celtic."

"It's not Celtic. I don't know why, but she was lying to us." He pointed to the words on the page. "That's what it says, right here. *Journal d'un voyageur.* A traveler's journal. It's in French."

"French? How do you know?" She leaned closer and examined the curlicues. How could Mrs. Winggen have been so wrong in her judgment? She was European, after all. Birdie would have thought she'd be more aware of the difference in languages.

"The script is old, so it's hard to make out, but even I can recognize the words as French. I studied it a little in school."

"What else does it say?" She turned the brittle paper to reveal more of the tiny script.

He inspected the page, moving the book closer to his face to get a better look. "I'm not sure. I can make out words – it looks like something to do with the coast – *la côte* – but we would need help to translate it completely."

"We'd better be careful with it," Birdie said. "It's so fragile now."

Ben turned to the next page and found it awash with the same tiny writing. They were a quarter of the way through the book before they saw what had been there the night before – the first page of *The Game and Playe of the Chesse*.

"It's as if someone added pages, sewed them in somehow," Birdie said. "But who? And how?"

"And when. The only time this thing was out of my sight was when I was sleeping." He examined the binding. "But you're right about the pages being sewn in. I think that's exactly what happened. For some reason, someone wanted to use this book to hide a journal." He closed it, wrapped it, and slipped it into the pocket of his cargo shorts.

"So now what?" he said.

"Let's go to Kayla's bookstore."

CHAPTER NINETEEN

Books and Tea was tucked along a string of storefronts on a curve of a lane in an area of Bruges that was more residential than touristy. The buildings rose four skinny stories, with shops facing the street and apartments on the upper floors. They backed up to one of the many canals, where double barn doors swung open to accept deliveries by boat.

The door to the small shop was painted the color of a blue jay and featured two stained-glass panels depicting storybook scenes. They were smaller than the windows at Mrs. Winggen's, but just as beautiful. A heady aroma of old leather and patchouli greeted Ben and Birdie as the door closed behind them, winking out the bright day.

Inside, narrow shelves crammed with all manner of books climbed toward the towering ceiling, where cobwebbed chandeliers hung dim and motionless. The shelves were filled with volumes of all shapes and sizes.

"Whoa," Ben said.

Birdie took a few steps down the center aisle and stopped. "I don't even know where to begin."

Ben surveyed the space. "There doesn't seem to be much logic in it."

Indeed, there was no rhyme or reason to it at all. She ran her hand across the uneven bindings of books in several languages, their names and topics and authors randomly stacked together.

"Looking for something in particular, then?"

Birdie turned on her heel and faced a bespectacled girl in her late teens dressed in a black skirt and scarlet top, each cut to reveal a world of colorful tattoos on her lanky arms and legs. Her blond hair was clipped short except for one long lock that swung low across her forehead in a brilliant shade of blue that matched her eyes, which sparkled beneath the heavy black frames of her glasses. A handmade name tag fashioned from tiny crystals was pinned just below her collar. It read Gretchen.

"Yes, we are, actually," Birdie said.

"Chess," Ben added. "We're looking for books on chess."

"Ah ha!" Gretchen pushed her glasses up the bridge of her nose. "A popular topic here, to be sure." She waved them deeper into the store. "Follow me."

She led them through the towering stacks, skirting several piles of haphazardly arranged books on the wooden floor. They descended a dark set of stairs at the far end of the shop, and exited in another part of the store where, unlike the jumble above, someone had taken a considerable amount of time and care to arrange books in various categories. At the far end of the room, wall-to-wall windows welcomed the sunlight and provided a lovely view of the sparkling canal beyond.

"Why is chess a popular topic here?" Birdie asked as they passed an orderly display of books related to Belgian chocolate making. The cover photos made her stomach rumble.

"Because of the books, of course," Gretchen said. "You know, the first books?"

They looked at her blankly.

Gretchen's colorful shoulders fell as she recited a story that Birdie could tell she'd told many times before.

"In 1472, an Englishman named William Caxton became a partner in a printing shop in Bruges using technology he'd learned in Germany from Herr Gutenberg. He translated and printed the first ever book in English, right here, in Bruges. It was called *The Recuyell of the Historyes of Troye*."

She pointed to a display featuring cutouts of Greek soldiers. They were pointing to tall stacks of neatly arranged leather-bound books. Several customers were standing around the table, paging through them.

Ben and Birdie exchanged glances. That was the book Kayla said her grandparents had been so interested in.

"It was hugely popular, so he translated and printed a second book in English called *The Game and Playe of the Chesse*. That was the last book in English he ever printed here, as France, Belgium, and England got themselves all mixed up in a conflict and he switched to printing in French and then some time in 1476 had uprooted himself and his press and moved to London."

"Did you say *The Game and Playe of the Chesse*?" Birdie

wanted to make absolutely sure she'd heard her correctly.

"Yes, that's right," Gretchen said. "We have them. This way."

They rounded a table featuring a skull-and-crossbones display of a book called *Bruges la Morte*.

"Dead," Ben mouthed to Birdie, pointing a thumb back at the table.

They followed Gretchen through the room, weaving past a variety of artfully arranged displays until they were in front of one with chess boards, figurines, and, as the foundation of it all, a stack of leather-bound books with a golden chess piece stamped on the front.

"It's not exactly a chess manual, even though that's what it sounds like," she said. "It's more of a moral guide, with examples of how people were supposed to behave using chess as an organizing principle. Yes, right. Here you are, then."

Before they could thank her, Gretchen was making her way back through the room and up the stairs.

"Told you he stole it," Ben said, so only Birdie could hear.

"I'm not so sure." She studied the display. The golden knights on the covers sparkled in the sun coming through the tall windows.

"I am."

"Well, they look like our book, but they're not the same." She picked a copy up and handed it to Ben. It was a fraction of the weight of the book in his pocket.

"Yeah, okay, I see what you mean. So then it's more likely he nipped it from the Begijnhof. I bet they have all kinds of old stuff there."

He opened the book. "It's the same text, with simple black-and-white illustrations. No handwriting."

"How much does it cost?"

He turned the book over and looked at the sticker on the back. "Wow. Twenty-five euros."

Birdie rummaged in her daypack.

"What are you doing?"

"I think we should buy one."

"What? Why? That's a lot of money."

"I'd like to compare it to the one we have," she said. "And the only other option is to steal it."

"Like the kid did."

"Exactly."

He dug deep into his cargo shorts and pulled out a few wrinkled bills and some coins. "Here's what I have."

"Thanks." She combined the two piles of cash on top of one of the chessboards and counted them out. "We should have enough to buy the book and still get something for lunch." She looked around the store. "Now where's Gretchen?"

CHAPTER TWENTY

With their new purchase in a paper bag and their old find securely in Ben's pocket, they made their way back outside.

"Let's try that place." Birdie pointed to a sandwich shop a few doors down on the quiet street. They ordered at the counter and then found a shady table out front to wait for their lunch.

Ben shook his head and laughed as he settled his tall frame onto the tiny metal chair. "This is so weird."

"Which part?"

"All of it. The books. This place. This day. I mean, look around."

They were squeezed onto a slip of sidewalk on a narrow cobblestone lane, surrounded by ancient buildings, as if this was something they did every day.

"Not what you're used to?"

"Uh, no. Are you? Getting a sandwich in Marshall Falls means a trip through the drive-thru."

"No," she admitted. "This is nothing like home. The

closest thing I've ever done was take a field trip to Philadelphia. They have some cobblestone streets, but it's not like this, a whole town preserved like it was the Middle Ages."

"See, there you go," he said. "Did you even know what the Middle Ages were before you came here?"

"Not really."

"I didn't. The closest I ever came was playing cloak-and-dagger video games."

Now it was her turn to laugh. "You're right. It's like a village in a video game."

"Do you play?" Ben's eyes brightened.

"Sometimes. But not for a while."

This was true. The video game console she'd once fought to get time on had sat dormant for more than a year, and was now packed in a storage unit across the Atlantic.

"I play all the time at home. I can disappear into my room and get away from my parents."

That sounded familiar. Jonah had spent hours in the basement playing video games, although they were more likely to be about sports than medieval quests.

"Speaking of getting away from your parents, I'm totally amazed that my mom is letting me walk around without her. It's definitely a first."

"Why? You're fifteen, right?"

"I turned fifteen in March, so not by much."

"She must think it's safe here."

"I guess." She glanced up and down the lane. There was certainly nothing to be afraid of on this street in broad daylight. "But she's really careful at home. I'd never be allowed to walk around our town alone."

"Your mom said it's a college town, right?"

"Yes. It has a different vibe than this place."

"Every place has a different vibe than this place. Besides, it's not like either of us is wandering the streets by ourselves. We're together. And we're what? Four blocks from your mom?"

"That's true." And if she thought about it, she'd been allowed to go off with Jonah sometimes, at the amusement park or the beach.

"So, where's your brother? Why didn't he come?" Ben asked, as if he were reading her thoughts.

A young woman with dark hair clipped into a messy bun delivered their sandwiches and two bags of chips – she called them crisps – on thin plates. Ben's was twice the size of Birdie's.

"I love these baguettes." He took a large bite.

"The bread is good," Birdie agreed. "It's another thing that's not like home."

"Have you even seen a plain old piece of white bread here?"

"No. But my mom never buys white bread at home, either."

"I love white bread. But I think I love this more." He took another giant bite of his sandwich.

When he finished chewing, he repeated his question about her brother.

She took a deep breath.

"My brother died last year. With my dad." Her voice cracked, but for once the tears stayed at bay. "They were in a terrible car accident."

Ben stopped chewing and sat back in his chair.

"It's okay," she continued. "We're okay. We're going to be okay. Everything is just... different now."

"I'm sorry, Birdie."

She saw the pain, the pity, in his eyes.

She knew that look. It was usually followed by horrible questions or some nervous excuse to get away from her, as if being too close would cause that person's family to die too.

"Me too," she said as she picked at her sandwich.

Ben worked his way through his bag of chips in silence. Birdie figured he was trying to think of a polite way to pull the ripcord on the whole day.

Instead, he said, "My parents are getting a divorce."

Now it was his turn to take a deep breath.

"They won't admit it to me, but I know what's going on. They basically hate each other. They used to fight all the time, but now they barely even talk to each other, which is worse if you ask me."

"I'm sorry, Ben," Birdie said. "That really stinks."

"Yeah, it does. They're pretty preoccupied with their problems. I got in trouble with some kids in town and they basically couldn't deal with it without screaming at each other, so they sent me here with Uncle Noah. Out of sight, out of mind, right?"

"Have you talked to them at all?"

"Not really. Uncle Noah sent them a couple of emails to let them know where we are, but that's about it."

"When do you go back to Texas?"

Ben let out a deep breath filled with what sounded like

relief. "Not for a long time. We'll be in Europe until the end of August, assuming Uncle Noah and I don't kill each other first. He's dead serious about this brewery thing and he's trying to pack five years of education into a three-month trip."

Two moms pushed strollers along the cobblestones and past the café, deep in conversation and oblivious to their babies' heads rattling along.

"What about you? How long are you staying?"

"We're spending the summer too." She took a bite of her sandwich and finished chewing before she continued. "I'll go back in time for school to start in the fall. We're hoping our house will be sold by then and we can move somewhere new."

"You mean you don't know where you'll live when you go home?"

"Nope, not yet anyway. Mom says we can always rent a place in town if the timing gets too tight. She doesn't want to pull me out of school."

"That makes sense."

"I thought so, too, but to be honest, now that I'm here, I'm not so sure. I'm not looking forward to going back."

"Why not?"

"Everything is different now. Everyone is different."

Ben considered her for a moment.

"Well, we don't have to go back today." He pushed their empty plates to one side of the table. "Let's take a look at those books again.

CHAPTER TWENTY-ONE

Birdie used a napkin to swipe the last of the crumbs onto the sidewalk as Ben wrested the book from his pocket. He placed it on the table next to the plain paper bag with the new version in it.

"They are definitely not the same thing." She withdrew the new copy from the bag and lined it up next to the old one.

Ben picked up the newer version and flipped through it. "It's a black-and-white copy of the old book. The text and illustrations are the same, but you can tell the pages were printed using different methods. This one is clean and crisp. Look at the ink in the old book. It's bled into the page and made the letters fuzzy."

"The ink wasn't like that yesterday. I swear yesterday it was almost as crisp as the new one." She lifted the fragile cover to reveal the first handwritten page. "Are you sure you don't know what this says?"

He peered at the tiny cursive. "I can tell it's a journal, and I can make out some words, but I'd have to study it and maybe use a translator app to understand it. The writing is just so old."

"What if it disappears?"

"The book?"

"Maybe, but no, I meant the journal pages," she said. "They weren't there when we found it. What if the next time we look, they're gone again?"

"Seems unlikely."

"It seems unlikely that they're there at all."

"True." Ben thought for a moment, and then his eyes brightened. "You have a camera in your bag, don't you?"

"Yes, I do." She felt inside the patchwork sack for the camera. "That's a great idea." She handed it to him. "No flash."

He gestured to the sunny day. "Shouldn't need it."

Birdie held each page open as he lined it up in the lens and snapped a picture, stopping to check each one to make sure it wasn't blurry.

When they were done, he handed the camera back to her. "Now it doesn't matter if the pages disappear. We can still try to figure out what they say."

"And we shouldn't have to open the book again. I'm worried we'll damage it. The corners of the pages want to snap off because they're so brittle. It was one thing when it seemed new, but now it's too fragile to keep messing with."

"Agreed." He wrapped the old book in its protective paper and returned it to his pocket.

Birdie checked her watch. "You know, when we were on

our way to Mrs. Winggen's house, we passed a sign for a library. We probably have just enough time to walk over there and see if we can use a computer."

"For what?"

"To translate some of those pages."

He nodded. "Not a bad idea. Let's do it."

"Hey, wait a minute," she said a few minutes later when they turned down a deserted lane.

Ben stopped walking. "What?"

"I want to try something. Do you see how skinny this lane is?"

"Yeah."

Birdie glanced up and down the street to make sure there were no cars or bicycles coming. "Spread your arms as wide as you can."

"Do what now?"

"Oh, just do it." She stood a couple of feet away from him and spread her arms wide. Her fingertips just touched the stone facade of the house on her side of the lane. Ben matched his fingertips to her outstretched hand and reached for the crumbling red brick house on the opposite wall.

"Not quite." He stretched his lanky limbs.

"No." She grinned. "But close!"

"You're funny." Ben dropped his arms. "Now come on before we get creamed by a cab."

They made their way through the twisting lanes to a low stone bridge. They crossed, then took a seat on the canal wall. Birdie pulled out her mom's map. "It was right around here somewhere. I remember seeing the sign."

Ben read over her shoulder as she studied the map. "There it is." He pointed to the words "*Bibliotheek*/Library," then glanced around to get his bearings. "We should be able to walk down that lane over there and then hang a right. We're close."

"Okay." She folded the map and put it back in her pocket. As she did, her fingers brushed against the piece of glass.

She pulled it out so Ben could see it. She rubbed it, but the knight held tight.

"It doesn't match anymore," he said. "The knight on the cover is a mix of colors now."

"It's like the gold is faded with age. One thing's for sure, the knight on the aventurine doesn't want to budge." She rubbed it again, and the glass grew warmer.

"I guess it only had that one trick," Ben said. "To go from the flower to the knight."

"It was just so cool when it changed."

He sat back and crossed his arms behind his head. "That it was."

Birdie followed his gaze up to the blue sky and then back to the row of medieval homes in front of them.

"Ben."

"What?"

"Do you see where we are?"

He looked up and down the lane. "Sure, we're by Mrs. Winggen's..."

"Yes. Look at the flowers."

"Huh?"

"The flowers. In Mrs. Winggen's window box. They're

red and purple again. Bright red and purple."

Ben lowered his arms. "You're right. I didn't notice when we sat down."

"Me neither. Let's go."

She hopped off the wall and started down the lane.

"Uh, Birdie, we can't bug that poor woman again," he said, jogging to catch up to her. "She's sure to tell Mrs. Devon and then Uncle Noah will find out."

"Just come on."

A moment later, they were standing in front of the red brick house.

"Look at the flowers."

"Yeah, they're great. Birdie—"

"Oh my gosh, there she is!"

"Who?"

"The girl. In the window."

Ben stepped back so he could see the eaves. A young girl stared down at him, her blond hair fanned in wide waves around her tiny face.

Birdie waved.

And the girl waved back.

"Mrs. Winggen lied to us," Ben said.

"Yep."

"So, who is she?"

"No clue."

"Do you think she's a prisoner?" He tented his hand over his brow as he stared at the window. "That Mrs. Winggen is keeping her? Making her clean the house or something?"

"No idea."

"We should call the cops. We're lucky we got out of there

alive."

A mewing at their feet drew their attention from the window. An orange and yellow tabby cat wound through their legs, nudging and purring.

"Go away, cat," Ben said, shooing it gently with his sneaker. He looked back at the window. "She's gone."

"What? No, wait. She's still there," Birdie said. "I can just make out her shadow."

A whistle sounded at the end of the block, and the cat slinked toward it. Birdie followed its silky movement and discovered the source of the whistle.

"It's him." She took a step forward.

Ben touched her shoulder. "Careful. Let's not scare him away again."

"He doesn't look scared." In fact, he was trotting toward them, sort of shimmering as he approached. She slipped the warm aventurine back into her pocket.

"Mon livre," he called as soon as he was close enough for them to hear. He continued forward until he stood right in front of them.

He was about the same height as Birdie, which meant Ben towered over them both. His eyes were green with flecks of blue, framed by sandy blond hair falling in loose waves across his forehead and nearly brushing his shoulders.

This close, she realized he was her age. She'd thought he was younger, but now she realized he was not. And he wore the same odd attire, this time with leather boots that resembled moccasins without the fringes. Like his pants, the shoes sagged as if they were too big.

"I'm sorry. I don't understand. Do you speak English?"

Birdie asked.

"His book," Ben said.

The boy nodded. *"Un peu. Mon livre, s'il vous plaît."* He paused to form the words. "A little. My book... please."

His accent was thick, as if he knew only a few words in English.

"How do we know it's yours?" Ben asked.

"How do you know we have it?" Birdie tried to enunciate her words.

The boy took a moment to process what she'd said. *"Je vous vois dans le parc.* I saw you in the park."

Then Ben said, *"Oui, nous avons trouvé le livre dans le parc. C'est votre?"*

Birdie's jaw dropped. "What did you just ask him?"

Ben grinned at her.

"I thought you said you didn't know French?"

His smile widened. "I told him we found the book in the park and asked if it's his."

"Oui," the boy replied, nodding vigorously. *"J'ai caché le livre. C'est à moi."*

"He says he hid it in the park and it's his."

Birdie didn't know if she was more surprised by Ben or the boy.

The boy held out his hand.

"Ask him what his name is."

"My name," the boy said slowly, clearly proud he'd understood her question, "is Henri."

"Bonjour, Henri." She repeated the name as he'd said it, sounding like *on-ree.* She was grateful she at least knew how to say hello in French. "My name is Birdie, and this is Ben."

Henri looked at Ben. He shook his outstretched hand. *"Mon livre, Ben, s'il vous plaît."*

Ben opened the flap of his shorts pocket and reached inside for the book.

"Hey, look," he said as he unwrapped the paper. The knight on the cover was bright gold again, and the book looked new.

Before she could respond, a high-pitched horn blasted behind them in the narrow lane. She jumped up on the stoop next to Ben. They flattened themselves against it as a BMW zoomed past.

"Maniac!" Birdie yelled after it, her heart racing.

They stepped down onto the cobblestones.

"Where did he go?" Ben turned in a circle in the middle of the lane.

Birdie tipped her head back and closed her eyes. "You've got to be kidding."

"Henri!" Ben yelled. "Damn it! He's gone again."

Birdie pivoted around. She saw a few wayward tourists, but no sign of the boy.

"Henri!" she called into the crowd.

"Don't bother, Birdie. He's gone."

Ben pointed to the house in front of them.

The flowers had faded to pink and yellow.

CHAPTER TWENTY-TWO

"So, you can't read French, huh?" Birdie said as they made their way back to the bed-and-breakfast, the trip to the library forgotten in the excitement of meeting Henri.

Ben laughed. "Well, I couldn't read the French in that book. Did you see how old it was? It was like reading Middle English."

"Well, you sure spoke to Henri with no problem."

"I know a little."

"Where did you learn it?"

"My parents sent me to a special preschool and one thing they taught us was a foreign language. I was in the section of kids that learned some French. It stuck in my brain okay. Last year they started offering it in school, so I got a refresher. I did pretty well, so I started practicing on my own. Did you know there are free language apps? I don't know that much, but I can get by with easy words. I've been trying to learn at least the basics for every country we're visiting."

"You sounded like you knew enough to me. My school

doesn't even offer French. It's Spanish or nothing."

"Our school is pretty big. So there are lots of choices. But not many kids take French. There were only about ten students in my class. All girls except for me. The school will probably drop it soon."

"Well, I'm glad they didn't drop it yet."

"Yeah, me too."

"We need to figure out some way to get that book to Henri," she said. "This is getting nuts."

"I know, and I can't stop thinking about that little girl. Why was she up in that room?"

"Maybe I should tell my mom about her."

"Do you think she'd believe you?"

"I don't know. And I can't be sure the girl would be around even if my mom did believe me and we went back to Mrs. Winggen's house."

Ben twisted his lips.

"What?"

He stopped walking and turned to her. "It's just that everything keeps shifting. It's like we're seeing things. The girl is there, then she's not. Henri wants the book but never sticks around long enough to get it. And why is he all dressed up if there are no reenactors in the summer anymore?"

"Mrs. Winggen could have been wrong about that. I saw a whole group of boys in period costumes when we were on the canal cruise."

"Okay, so say she is wrong. That still doesn't explain why the heck the flowers keep changing colors."

"I've been thinking about the flowers," Birdie said. "If Mrs. Winggen is keeping those kids against their will, maybe the flowers are some kind of signal. Maybe they weren't replanted at all, but she's switching out the pots—"

"Or the little girl is." Ben sucked in a breath. "Or, maybe she's not the only one up there. Whatever's going on we need to try to help her. If we can't tell your mom, maybe we could wait until Mrs. Winggen leaves and sneak through the back door or something."

"I don't know about that."

"Well, do you have any better ideas?"

She thought for a moment. "Not right now. But give me some time. Maybe I'll come up with something."

"Better make it quick. Time is something we're short on."

When they arrived at the bed-and-breakfast, it was nearly time for Uncle Noah to return.

"I'm going to see if my mom's back."

"Do you want the book?"

"No, you hold on to it. I can't read it, anyway."

"Let me see your camera. Maybe I can use Uncle Noah's phone to translate those handwritten pages. We're supposed to go to a place called the Monk Bar tonight for dinner. Maybe he'll let me out of it."

She shrugged. "Okay, but I doubt it since you spent the day with us. But let me know if you discover anything." She reached into the pocket of her jeans and pulled out the piece of glass. "Here. Hold on to this too. Maybe the handwriting says something about it."

"Are you sure?" He eyed the aventurine.

"I'm sure. You can give it back to me tomorrow before we leave."

He turned the cool piece of glass over in his palm.

"Still the knight," he said.

Birdie nodded. "Okay, see you tomorrow."

He unlocked the door to the room he shared with his uncle on the first landing, and she continued up the stairs to the attic.

"There you are," her mom said as Birdie came into the sunny room and kicked off her sneakers. "I was thinking I might need to call in a search party."

"Sorry. Have you been here long?"

"No. I'm just kidding. I got back ten minutes ago."

"How was lace-making?"

"Hard. But I made this." She held up a piece of white lace about the size of a coffee coaster. The delicate threads formed a flower pattern in the center of the piece.

"It's pretty. You made it?"

"I did. It took me all afternoon. You should see the older women do this. They move so fast. Their hands are like little machines. For every one loop I made, they made at least seven or eight."

"Wow."

"I got some sketching done, too, during the breaks." She showed Birdie a design for a wall hanging that resembled the arched windows of a church. She was getting the hang of the stained glass. The drawing reminded Birdie of the lion and the bear in the door in Mrs. Winggen's vestibule.

"It looks great," Birdie said. Her mom came alive again when she was working on designs. It was the only time the shadows completely lifted around her. "So, what's on the agenda for tonight?"

"Not much. I figured we'd find a little bistro for dinner and then come back here. I'd like to get some more work done."

"Sounds good to me." Actually, it sounded great. She flopped onto the edge of the bed.

"How was your day with Ben?"

"Good. The bookstore was neat."

Her mom nodded, but she could tell she'd refocused on her sketch. Birdie settled against her bed pillow.

"Oh, and I decided we'd leave a little later tomorrow instead of first thing in the morning. I want to go to the church to see the Michelangelo statue again. We were so tired and rushed when we were there the first time. I'm not sure I really gave it the attention it deserved. We're driving, so we have some flexibility about when we leave."

"We're going to Germany?"

"Yes. To the Rhine and Mosel Rivers. There are some old castles there I want to check out."

"Castles, really?"

She looked up again and smiled. "Really."

"Cool," Birdie said.

Bruges is generally safe, even on the back lanes late at night.

—*Marty McEntire,* Europe for Americans Travel Guide

CHAPTER TWENTY-THREE

Birdie tossed the warm duvet from her legs and sat up. The attic was dark except for a patch of moonlight that fell across her bed through the open window.

A sound like gravel kicking up from a truck tire sputtered beneath the windowsill. She'd been listening to the noise in her dreams for what seemed like hours, hitting the wall and scattering again and again.

On the other side of the room, her mom's breathing was steady and smooth.

Birdie dropped her bare feet to the cool wooden planks and slipped silently from the bed.

The noise sounded again.

She stepped to the window and peered outside, expecting to see gravel on the windowsill, but nothing was there.

Shadows danced along the cobblestone lane as the wind blew dark clouds across the sky, an undulating mass of gray and black slipping over and past the moon.

Flowers fluttered in the window boxes along the narrow

street, and an errant sheet of newspaper lifted and dipped, following the current toward the arched intersection.

It felt like ages since she'd slipped under that arch with her mom, so worried about beating the clock to reach the keypad before the code changed.

A rush of cold air crossed her warm skin. She shivered as she listened, waiting.

Nothing.

Had she imagined the noise? Had it been in her dream, after all?

She checked the clock on the nightstand.

Half-past two.

This was ridiculous. She glanced one last time at the lane below.

She gasped, then covered her mouth to silence herself.

Henri and the little girl stood near the corner where the alley flowed into the lane. The tabby cat sat properly by the girl's feet, which were barely visible beneath her long dress. They were staring at her window, almost shimmering in the silvery light.

Birdie raised her hand in acknowledgment.

Henri cupped his hand, gesturing for her to come down to the street. As he did, another gust of wind whistled through, stirring old leaves from the window boxes into a whirlwind that flew skyward in tight formation until the air it rode on stopped. The leaves hung suspended for an instant before drifting down to the cobblestones.

Henri motioned to her again.

What was she doing? She did not want to be out after dark.

The shutters and windows of the surrounding houses were drawn. No one else was watching, witnessing the long shadows thrown by Henri, the girl, and the tabby as they waited for her.

She shook her head.

No. She was not going downstairs, not going outside in the middle of the night.

She backed away and sat down on the edge of the bed. She closed her eyes and willed Henri and the girl to disappear.

Gravel rattled again across the windowsill.

Her heartbeat quickened.

No. She'd never get past her mom. Even if she did, she'd be in such trouble if she got caught.

And what if she did go down there and it was all for nothing?

What if she got down there and Henri was gone?

He had a bad habit of disappearing.

She stepped back to the window. They were still there, waiting.

Henri beckoned her again, more urgently.

She hesitated.

What if Ben was right and Mrs. Winggen was holding the girl? What if Henri had rescued her? What if he'd brought her here, to t'Bruges Huis, so Birdie could call the police?

What if she was their only hope?

She considered the girl, so small in the night. She must be terrified.

She couldn't just stand here in the dark doing nothing.

Should she wake her mom?

She glanced behind her.

No. She would not disturb her when she was finally sleeping soundly. Not for what was probably a wild goose chase.

She snatched her jeans and jacket from the floor beside the bed. Her hands shook as she slid them on; her heartbeat felt audible in the quiet night.

She tiptoed across the attic, willing herself to be light and invisible.

She was halfway across the room when her mom shifted under the covers and her breath changed rhythm.

Birdie froze mid-step and closed her eyes.

If she got caught now, she could just say she was going to the bathroom.

Right.

The bathroom.

She opened her eyes.

A noise like a horse and carriage rattling past floated through the room from the open window. Birdie raced to the door, her movement disguised by the sound outside. She picked up her sneakers and paused, listening.

Her mom's breath was steady again.

The key hung from the lock and she twisted gingerly until it made one full rotation and the door popped open an inch. She opened it far enough to slip through, dashed into the dark hallway, and closed it again. She scanned the ceiling for the white dot that activated the motion sensor, spotted it at the far end of the stairwell, then flattened herself against the wall as she maneuvered down the steps to avoid triggering it.

She landed each footfall with care, mindful of the creaky

stairs. She reached the landing, rounded the corner, and slid past Ben's room. She longed to wake him, but there was no way to manage it without knocking on his door and waking the rest of the house – and Uncle Noah – at the same time.

She continued down the hall to the second landing.

Halfway there. There was no way she'd make it all the way down to the foyer.

But she did.

Almost.

She stood pinned against the mirrored wall two steps above the mosaic floor, her sneakers dangling from her hand, and studied the dark foyer. There was no way to reach the front door and open it without tripping the light sensor.

She winced as she barreled across the tiny tiles, shielding her eyes against the explosion of light from the chandelier. She opened the heavy door as quickly and quietly as she could and skidded out onto the stoop, her heart hammering against her ribs and her legs shaking.

She closed her eyes again and took a few deep, steady breaths.

They sounded ragged, but she knew that was normal. The grief counselor had trained her to breathe to fight the panic attacks that plagued her in the first months after Jonah and her dad died. She whispered her mantra, inhaling and exhaling between each repetition.

"I am in no danger here."

"I am in no danger here."

"I am in no danger here."

She never imagined she'd be using her counselor's advice to sneak out of the house.

She bet the counselor never imagined it, either.

But it was working, and she felt herself calm.

"I am in no danger here," she whispered.

As her heartbeat settled, she opened her eyes. Her vision had adjusted to the night and she could easily make out everything by the light of the moon.

She yanked her sneakers on without bothering to untie them, then examined the deserted lane. As she did, another gust of wind whistled through it. She pulled her jacket tighter and zipped it up.

There was no sign of Henri or the little girl – or even the cat.

"Seriously?" she whispered. "Where are you guys?"

A curtain shifted in a second-story window across the lane. She caught the movement from the corner of her eye but didn't look up.

She had to decide. She couldn't stay mounted on the stoop like a potted plant forever.

This was not smart. It was probably the dumbest thing she'd ever done. But she was already outside and would be in big trouble if she got caught. She might as well try to figure out what Henri wanted, see if he'd left a clue in the alley. Maybe she could help.

She tucked her hands in her jacket pockets, bowed her head, and stepped off the stoop, watching her footing on the uneven cobbles. She ignored the houses that lined the lane, not wanting to know what lurked there, behind the drawn curtains and shuttered windows.

She turned into the dark alley where the children and the cat had stood watching her. She had no idea how much time had passed since she'd spotted them from the window.

One thing was for sure: there was no sign of them now.

She scanned the cobblestones, searched for anything the children might have left behind.

Her gaze caught on a shiny object a few inches away.

As she bent to retrieve it, a firm hand gripped her elbow.

CHAPTER TWENTY-FOUR

"Birdie, shush. It's me."

Ben.

She twisted in his grasp, using her free hand to push him hard in the chest. "I almost screamed my head off. You scared me half to death!"

He didn't move, but his angular face brightened with surprise.

"Ah, come on. I wasn't going to let you come out here alone. Besides, I thought you had something against sneaking out."

"I… Henri…" She tried to motion down the alley, but Ben still had hold of her arm.

"Yeah. I saw them too," he said, dropping his hand now that he could be sure she wouldn't scream and wake up the neighborhood. "No sign of them now, though."

"Did you bring the book?" She searched the street for any trace of the other children. She tried to pick up the shiny object but found it was just a marking on a cobblestone.

Ben patted the pocket of his camouflage shorts.

"How many pairs of cargo shorts do you own?"

He smiled his crooked smile. "Is there any other kind?" He retrieved the aventurine from his back pocket. "Here. Before I forget." He handed it to her. "I'll give you the camera at breakfast. Uncle Noah made me go to that Monk Bar, so I hardly had any time to use the computer. I was trying to find something about the knight when I heard Henri throwing rocks at the windows."

"Thanks," she said as he dropped the warm aventurine on her palm. "Okay, so what are we going to do? We need a plan."

"Well, we're out now. If we get caught we'll be in deep sh—"

"Yeah, I know."

"So we might as well make it worthwhile." He started down the alley, and she fell into step beside him.

"Where are you going?"

"Not sure."

A few minutes later, they came to the bend in the canal. To Birdie's surprise, Henri was there, crouched against the wall with the little girl tucked up behind him.

"Oh, thank God," she whispered.

As they drew closer, she smiled at the girl, whose wavy blond bangs fell into green eyes that looked like Henri's.

"I have the book." The Velcro flap on his shorts produced a ripping noise as he opened it. *"J'ai la livre."*

Henri held out his hand.

"It's strange." Ben pulled the volume free from the fabric. "The book changed..."

Snarling rose behind them.

Birdie felt her heart in her throat as she whirled around, her arms raised, expecting to fight off a wild dog.

What she saw instead made it almost stop beating altogether.

A shimmering pack of boys were snaking up the alley, carrying small bats and large rocks.

"LeFort!" a tall one roared. His nose looked like it had been broken and poorly reset more than once.

"Aide moi!" Henri whispered to Ben, his eyes pleading. Then he turned to the girl. *"Cours, Marguerite! Cours!"*

Henri and Marguerite sprinted up the alley, banking in opposite directions at an intersection several yards away.

Ben gripped Birdie's shoulder and pulled her up onto the stoop of a darkened house. They ducked behind a pair of lion statues that guarded the front door.

The boys rumbled past, yelling and cursing as if Ben and Birdie weren't there.

"It's like they didn't even see us," she said.

"Come on!" Ben jumped from the stoop and chased after the boys as they turned down the path Henri had taken.

"What did Henri say to you?" she gasped as they ran at full speed.

"Help. He asked for help."

Birdie ran harder.

They reached the end of the lane, turned onto a major street, and then banked into another alley, chasing the sound of the boys' soft-soled shoes as they slapped against the cobblestones. The alley circled back to the canal where the slow-moving water reflected the moon as it slipped in and out of the clouds, creating a surreal nightlight in the mist.

They tucked in close to the stone wall that traced the canal, the bulky figures of the boys, moving slower now, just visible far ahead in the dark.

"I hope he loses them," Birdie said, her breath coming in quick bursts.

"Me too."

"Those boys – they're trouble."

"You're telling me."

They crept along the wall, trying not to draw any attention. The boys had ignored them once. They might not be so lucky a second time.

The houses on the other side of the canal fell away, revealing a dark expanse. It was familiar, and she realized they were near the park where they'd first seen Henri.

"This way," Ben said.

They crouched low as they crossed a bridge and slipped into the Minnewater, following a path of crushed grass and skirting the tree where Henri had hidden the book. An open gate led to the Begijnhof, where a church towered above the overgrown courtyard, and shadows of windswept trees quivered against the whitewashed bungalows where the sisters slept.

They listened for the boys, but the courtyard was silent. The trickle of water in the canal, the whistling of the breeze through the tall grass, even the harshness of her own breath fell away, and time made space for peace.

Henri wasn't here, and neither was Marguerite, or those awful boys.

She wished she'd never left the safety of her warm bed. She touched Ben's shoulder. "Maybe we should turn back."

He pointed to the trampled grass that led through the courtyard to a second gate. "They're still here."

She hesitated. "What if we find them? If we catch up? What then?"

"We'll make sure Henri and Marguerite are okay."

"But…"

He swung around to face her. She took half a step back in surprise.

"But what?"

She peered into his eyes. Jonah had confronted her like this a million times. She'd always felt so small and stupid when he did. The words would never come.

But Ben wasn't looking at her like she was stupid. He was exasperated, to be sure, but not angry.

"Look," he said, spreading his hands wide, "I know you're scared. I'm a little freaked out too. But we started this and I think we should finish it."

"Return the book."

"Yes."

"And then we can go back to the bed-and-breakfast."

"And back to our normal, ordinary, safe lives."

Birdie took a deep breath.

Ben waited.

"Okay."

She stepped past him, leading the way to the far gate, which opened into another grassy area awash in moonlight. Benches and well-groomed hedges enclosed the circular space, and a fountain pulsed in the center. Two women made of stone forever watched the flow of the water. A white cottage with darkened windows stood sentinel on the far side.

The boys were there, milling in front of the cottage, searching.

A brush of movement to their right caught Birdie's attention. A whisper of shadow drifted over the ground as Henri nudged Marguerite through a dark passage in the hedge. He glanced back toward the cottage, then disappeared behind her.

"Did you see…" Birdie's voice died in her throat as one of the boys called out using words she didn't understand but a tone she couldn't mistake.

They'd spotted Henri.

The boys barreled through the hedge, pushing and shoving.

Ben sprinted across the park with Birdie at his heels. She ducked through the hedge after him, her nostrils flaring with the sweet scent of pine needles. When she emerged on the other side, her shoulders were damp with dew.

She shivered as she took stock of an imposing building that loomed ahead, its weight supported by a series of Gothic arches.

Henri and Marguerite darted toward it, but the boys were gaining on them.

Birdie held her breath, not wanting to watch but unable to turn away.

They would never outrun them.

Suddenly, Henri scooped Marguerite into his arms and ducked into one of the archways. Their figures faded to black, as if they'd disappeared.

The boys pulled up short and scattered.

Ben and Birdie watched as they ran away.

"That was weird," she said.

"They didn't want to follow Henri in there, that's for dang sure."

"I wonder why?" She tilted her head and squinted, but saw only the void framed by each arch.

"Let's go find out."

"Are you serious?"

"If Henri took Marguerite in there, it can't be that bad."

She wasn't so sure, but she followed Ben anyway. Whatever was under those arches couldn't be any worse that being out here alone if those boys came back.

They crossed beneath the archway and entered a shallow alcove. It was empty except for a flight of crumbling stairs that corkscrewed down into blackness.

"They must have gone down," he said, angling his sneaker on the first step.

"Great." She waited until his head was no longer visible, then seized the railing and followed. She felt her way forward until she reached the bottom, where a massive wooden door blocked their progress.

She pushed past Ben and pulled the handle. To her surprise, it opened with ease.

*In the Middle Ages, many children left home at about
age ten for education or to go to work as servants.
Those who didn't have a father were assigned another
male relative to oversee their upbringing, or, if there were
no other male relatives, given to a male member of the
community the aldermen found acceptable.*

—*Marty McEntire,* Europe for Americans Travel Guide

CHAPTER TWENTY-FIVE

They crossed a rough-hewn threshold and the solid door drifted shut behind them. Ben sucked in a breath and Birdie drew her jacket up over her nose.

At first, before her eyes adjusted to the gloom, she guessed they'd landed in the dismal cellar of an ancient house, one with a floor made of dirt. But as her vision cleared, she realized it was not a cellar at all, but a vast underground chamber, where wide stone arches marched overhead, weaving a honeycomb of dark alcoves.

She was reminded of the Jerusalem Chapel, but without the soaring steeple to filter the moonlight. The only light here flickered from candles deep within the alcoves, illuminating air thick with smoke and smelling of mildew, well-cooked sausages, and something else that she preferred not to identify.

Henri emerged from the shadows of the alcove closest to the door. He gripped Birdie's wrist with surprising strength and she nearly dropped the aventurine she'd been holding.

"What are you doing?" she demanded as she passed it to her other hand and slipped it into the pocket of her jeans. She twisted her shoulder and wriggled her arm, but Henri held firm. "Let me go."

"Come." He pulled her deeper into the long chamber.

Birdie glanced over her shoulder at Ben, who was following close behind, ducking to clear each low arch. When one of her sneakers caught on the roughly cobbled floor, he leaned in to steady her.

"This is the Monk Bar," he whispered.

She knitted her brow.

This was no bar. There were no stools, no wooden tables like she'd seen at the café the other night. The floor was a disaster of uneven stones that even a sober person would struggle to navigate.

Up ahead, a weak campfire burned, its gray smoke floating to the ceiling where it hugged the arches before dissipating. Several boys about her age huddled at a table near it, bent over a game of dice. They sat back as Ben, Birdie, and Henri passed by.

The beefiest of the group, a young man with a face that resembled a deflated beach ball, sneered at Henri. He elbowed the kid next to him, whose hunched-over features reminded Birdie more of a rat than a boy.

"LeFort, the witch's daughter is coming." Rat Boy revealed pitted teeth as he spoke. "She will torture you in your sleep. Right, Jan?" He nudged the beefy boy next to him, who gave an ugly laugh.

"Do not look," Henri murmured so only Birdie could hear.

She did as he instructed, peering instead into each alcove they passed. The arches concealed dozens of children living amid mounds of clothes, blankets, and broken things. Many were sleeping, so thin they seemed more like piles of dirty rags than little humans.

Henri jerked her hard, and she stumbled, catching herself only when firm hands grasped her upper arms.

"Enough!" Birdie glared into the dull blue eyes of a teenage girl who stood slightly taller than she did. She was emaciated, but also quite strong, judging by the pain Birdie felt from her grip. "Let. Me. Go."

"Anglais," Henri said.

The older girl dropped her hands from Birdie's arms, and Henri released her wrist.

Birdie shook her arms and then rubbed the indentations on her wrist where his finger marks remained. "Was that really necessary?"

"Welcome," the girl said, her voice low and raspy in the smoky room.

"Who are you?" Ben stepped forward so he stood beside Birdie. "What's going on here?"

"Henri, leave us."

He bowed and stepped away.

The girl's straw-colored hair hung in a wide braid that reached her waist. She'd partially tucked it under a hat that reminded Birdie of a throw pillow. She wore thick leggings and a dark overcoat that dwarfed her slender form.

The candlelight revealed a modest, orderly space behind her. Frayed tapestries hugged each of the three walls, and a tattered duvet covered a bed made of wooden crates. On the far end, a large barrel served as a desk and a smaller one as a chair.

The candles threw a brighter light here, their thickness and quantity superior to those in the rest of the dungeon.

Dungeon, Birdie thought with a start.

She was in a dungeon with strange kids from Bruges. Did they do this often? Lure stupid tourists to their lair in the middle of the night and then do God knew what to them? What had she been thinking?

"I am Eva."

Birdie scanned the room for something she could use as a weapon. Her options were limited: a candlestick, a wooden barrel, a spool of twine.

She was glad for Ben beside her. They didn't speak, but she knew he was also strategizing an escape. It was a long way back to the door they entered, but perhaps there was another way out.

"Do you have a name?" Eva asked, drawing Birdie's attention back to her.

"My name is Birdie." She was grateful that her voice didn't quiver.

Eva stroked her braid and laughed, a hollow sound that echoed through the dark corridor and chilled Birdie to the bone.

"And you?" she asked, sizing Ben up. She surveyed him from head to toe and then cocked her head at his bare knees. "Is your name Fox?" She laughed again.

"We need to get back," Birdie said.

"Eva," Ben said evenly, "my name is Benjamin."

"Ah, he can speak. A proper Christian name too. But

what has happened to your trousers?" She'd stopped laughing, but a glint of humor teased her eyes. She turned to Birdie. "And you, my little swallow, where is your gown?"

Her questions were met with silence. Even the children in the alcoves were quiet. Birdie imagined them listening, waiting for a signal to know if she and Ben were friend or foe.

"Ah yes," Eva continued when they didn't respond. "You are curious why Henri brought you here?"

Birdie's eyes narrowed. Had he led them here on purpose? Had this been his plan all along, to trap them in this awful place? He'd be sorely disappointed if the goal was robbery. They'd spent every euro on lunch and the new chess book. The only thing in her pocket now was the aventurine.

She caught herself before she dug into her pocket to grasp it, to protect it. Such a move would alert everyone there was something valuable there. She stilled, but each nerve in her body sprang to attention.

"I asked," Eva said, edging closer to Birdie, "because I am curious about you. Henri tells me you appeared one day on the brewery roof. You just, appeared." She opened her hands as if she were tossing pixie dust into the air. "And then you" – she scanned Ben's tall frame – "you appeared too."

Silence stretched in the dim candlelight.

"Again you say nothing?" She leaned in close.

"We're on vacation," Birdie said, as if this was the most natural exchange she'd ever had.

"Vacation?" Eva rolled the word in her mouth.

"Yes. We're on... holiday. We're American."

Eva tilted her head back and laughed again.

The hair on Birdie's arms stood on end. "Why are you here? Hiding out?"

The laugh became a snarl. "We must hide, you fool. We may not walk freely like you."

"Why not?" Ben asked.

Eva scowled, as if she'd forgotten he was there. "If we are seen, they will take us before the aldermen, and if we are lucky, put us with a family that will work us to death. If we are not lucky, they will send us back from whence we came."

"From whence you came?" Birdie lifted her brows. "And where exactly did you come from? Why are you really here? Are you runaways? Where are your parents?" She glanced around the chamber, then dropped her voice low. "Or is someone holding you here?"

She dared a hard look at Ben. He was surveying the room, clearly searching for the best escape. They had to get out of here, and fast.

"We choose to be here." Eva dismissed the suggestion of captivity with a swish of her fingers. "It is our last choice. Our parents are dead. The plague left us at the mercy of the aldermen. Our city? It is dead too. The port no longer flows. Ships rarely come. The guilds and the merchants fight in the streets. Everyone is abandoning it, abandoning us. Only those who cannot leave have stayed."

Ben folded his arms across his chest. "Even if we did believe you, there's not a dang thing we can do about any of that."

"You can give me the book. It does not belong to you. Henri says you have his book."

"The chess book?" Ben said. "How could that help?

Besides, maybe we have it, and maybe we don't. Why's it so important?"

"It is ours. That is all you need to know." She didn't meet Ben's gaze when she spoke, but stared coldly into Birdie's.

"Well, I don't have it," Birdie said, only half-lying. It was in Ben's pocket, not hers. She took a step back. "Not with me anyway."

There was no way she was giving Henri's book to this girl. She didn't know what was going on, but she had to guess that Henri wouldn't have led them here if that gang of boys hadn't been on his tail. And now he was nowhere to be found.

"You will bring it to me," Eva said. "And Henri and Marguerite will continue to have my protection."

"We found the book in the park." Birdie shifted back another step. "What right do you have to it?"

"It is Henri's. Therefore, it is mine to protect. It belonged to his father."

"His father?" Ben asked. "What happened to his parents?"

Eva glared at him. "Have you not been listening? The sickness took them. It spared Henri and Marguerite, but only them."

"Why was Henri running from the old woman?" Birdie asked.

"Old woman?"

"At the park."

"Park?"

"Um, the Minnewater? A nun?"

"Ah. The beguine." Eva lowered her eyelids. "She thinks

the book belongs to her, but she does not need it."

"And you do?" Ben asked.

"Of course."

"For what?" Birdie asked.

Eva ignored the question. "You will bring it here. Tomorrow night."

Ben stood up taller. "Why should we—"

"Wait." Birdie held her hand up to stop him. Tomorrow night was perfect. She'd be well on her way to Germany by then. One thing was for sure at the moment, though – the promise of that leather-bound book was their ticket out of this place.

"Tomorrow night," she agreed. "We'll bring it to the park and leave it where we found it."

Eva cupped her hands around her mouth. "Henri!"

He skittered forward from the darkness.

"We are done here."

He bowed, then motioned for Ben and Birdie to follow him. As they passed an alcove, he ducked inside and retrieved Marguerite, who'd snuggled in with several other children on top of a pile of rags.

"Henri!" Eva called.

"*Oui?*"

"You will stay."

He swallowed, then led them away through the wooden door, up the spiral stairs, and out into the night. Birdie sucked in the fresh air, relieved to see there was no sign of the boys who'd been chasing Henri and Marguerite.

"*Le livre,*" Henri whispered, "it was my father's and it belongs to me. Not Eva. She will not protect it. She will steal it from me as payment even though I owe her nothing. She will sell it." He glanced over his shoulder. "To feed them."

He turned away and, clutching his young sister to his chest, disappeared down the stairwell, leaving them alone on the path.

The sky cleared momentarily, and the moon lit the way to the hedge.

Birdie and Ben exchanged glances.

Then, they ran.

CHAPTER TWENTY-SIX

"You did what?" Kayla demanded.

"Keep your voice down," Ben said.

Birdie had never seen Kayla show any emotion other than boredom, and certainly not anger. Before now, she would've said Kayla didn't care enough about anything or anyone to be angry.

Except maybe her phone.

"You could've been kidnapped or killed, you idiots."

"We were fine," Ben said. "And keep your voice down before you wake up the whole house."

"You should have told me you were going."

They were in a cramped bedroom on the second floor of t'Bruges Huis, two doors down from the room Ben shared with his uncle. It held one twin bed topped by a yellow duvet like the one in Birdie's room, a desk, a nightstand, and, from what Birdie could tell, a minuscule bathroom behind a flowered curtain that hung partly open. Kayla had scared them half to death when she cracked her door and ushered them inside as they made their way up the stairs.

Now Ben stood leaning against the wall with his long legs crossed at the ankles and his arms folded against his chest. Birdie sat in the chair at the desk.

"Why would we tell you?" he said. "You couldn't have cared less what we've been doing."

"Maybe if we'd made a YouTube video about it," Birdie said under her breath. Ben's mouth twisted, but he was too irritated with Kayla to laugh. When it came right down to it, they were both too relieved to be back at the bed-and-breakfast to care much about getting waylaid by Kayla.

"Well, I didn't know you were going to end up sneaking out." She slumped onto her bed. Birdie saw a pout flirt with her lips, but then she recovered. "You should have told me so I could've gone with you. You know, to protect you."

Now Ben did laugh.

"Trust me, we were fine," Birdie said.

"Where did you go?" Her sudden interest was unnerving.

"What are you doing up, anyway?" Ben asked.

Birdie was glad he avoided her question. This was none of Kayla's business.

She snatched her phone from the nightstand and held it up as if they were supposed to see something on the dark screen.

"I couldn't sleep. My friends back home are having so much fun. And here I am, stuck in this totally dead small town with Grammy and Gramps. I wish someone would just shoot me now."

"Bruges la morte," Ben said.

"What?" Kayla said.

"I don't know," Birdie said. "Your grandparents seem okay to me." She rarely saw her own grandparents, especially since the accident.

Kayla shot her a withering look. "You would think so."

"What's that supposed to mean?"

"Nothing. Now, out with it. Tell me where you were or I'll make up something juicy to tell your uncle and your mom."

"You wouldn't." Ben leaned forward.

"Try me," Kayla said, her blue eyes turning steely.

They stared at each other.

Finally, Birdie broke the standoff. "If you must know, we decided to return that book we found to the boy who dropped it."

"In the middle of the night?"

"Why not?" Ben held her gaze.

"Uh, because you're already in deep with your uncle and she's a Miss Goody Two-shoes who wouldn't sneak out unless she had a life-or-death reason."

"Guess you were wrong about me," Birdie said.

"Uh, doubtful. What kind of trouble are you two in, anyway?"

"We're not in any trouble," Ben said. "We just wanted to return the book before Birdie leaves in the morning."

"Speaking of which," she said, unable to stifle a yawn, "I need to get back upstairs before my mom realizes I'm out of bed."

Light from the hall spilled across the floor through the slit under the door.

"Too late." Kayla jumped up and pulled the door open before Ben or Birdie could protest. "Hi, Mrs. Blessing," she said. "She's in here."

Her mom stood in the doorway in her robe.

Birdie's mouth went dry.

"We were playing cards." Kayla pointed to a deck of cards on the table next to her bed.

Birdie yawned again. "Probably not the best idea," she said sheepishly, standing and following her mom into the hall.

"Probably not. Don't leave the room after lights out again, here or anywhere we stay. Do you understand?"

"Yes. Sorry, Mom." She didn't turn around, but she sensed Ben behind them. A moment later, she heard the nearly imperceptible sound of the door to his room closing.

Her mom left the conversation there. She was grateful for that and for the soft bed and the warm covers.

She crawled inside and slept.

It was Ben who woke her a few hours later, rather than her mother. He gripped the book in one hand and his uncle's cellphone in the other.

"How did you get in here?" Birdie asked, sitting up on her elbows.

"Your mom's downstairs having breakfast." He kept his voice low so the other guests wouldn't overhear him. "She left the door unlocked."

"But why…"

"Birdie, I was doing a little more research online. I think this book may be one of the original copies of *The Game and Playe of the Chesse* that was printed here in Bruges. That's the reason those kids want it – it's valuable and rare. Remember what the girl at the bookstore——"

"Gretchen."

"Yeah, okay, Gretchen. Do you remember what she said?"

"It's the second book ever printed in the English language."

"Exactly. The book was one of a handful printed by William Caxton, the first person to print books in English. He did it here in Bruges. He printed two books in English and then switched to French for a while before moving to England and switching back to English again."

"Eva said the book belonged to Henri's father."

"According to this, there are ten remaining copies that have been accounted for. There's a complete copy in the British Library in London, but all the others are incomplete. They're missing pages or damaged."

"So where did this one come from then?"

"I don't know, but listen to this. There's an old rumor, never confirmed, that the beguines once had a complete copy, but they lost it."

"The Begijnhof," Birdie said. "It belongs to the sisters. That's why the nun was chasing Henri. So he did steal it from there."

"It's looking that way. I can't think of another explanation."

"So we should return it to the nuns." Birdie lay her head back on the soft pillow.

Ben studied her for a moment.

"We should," he said slowly, "you're right. But I haven't told you everything. That website, the one that said the beguines had a copy? Well, it also said there's another rumor that the lost book hid a diary. And not just any diary. They think it held a secret to the riches of Venice."

"You're kidding."

"Maybe we should spend some time with it before we return it," he said.

"Venice?"

"Yes, Venice. Remember what Mrs. Winggen said? Bruges and Venice were the two big deal ports, the places where riches and treasures changed hands."

"The handwritten part..."

"That's what I was thinking, that the journal section could be about Venice."

"Did you get a chance to translate any of it?"

Ben shook his head.

"We don't have much time. My mom and I are leaving this afternoon." She sat up, yanking the duvet under her chin. "But don't you think the nuns would've examined this book inside and out if they knew it was supposed to contain that secret? What are we going to find that they didn't?"

"Good point. Still, it doesn't seem right to just hand it over to them. They clearly weren't taking very good care of it." He grinned. "We found it lying on the ground."

"Yeah, except that it belongs to them and not to us or to Henri. What if they think we stole it? We have to return it."

Ben sat at the foot of her bed and stared out the window for a while. He met her eyes and threw his hands in the air. "I got nothing."

"We could go back and ask Henri why he took it," Birdie said. "We could retrace our steps from last night."

"Do you really want to go back to that place?"

"No."

"Neither do I."

"But I'm not sure how else to find him again. His house is, well, unreliable with Mrs. Winggen there, and the dungeon was the last place we saw him."

"But Birdie..." He stopped when he heard a rustle of wings and air. He stood up. "What the?"

WOO who.

A dove lighted on the windowsill and bobbed its head at them.

WOO who.

"There's a... bird staring in here."

"Oh, that's just Willy. Don't worry about him. He won't come in."

"Willy?"

"He's been here every morning. He's a wood pigeon. I thought he was a dove, but he's a plain old pigeon. Apparently pigeons are a type of dove. Or maybe it's vice versa. I don't remember. At least that's what my mom said."

Ben stared at the bird as it bobbed its head. "He has straps on his leg."

"What do you mean?"

"Look, there are little leather straps on his leg, like he had something tied there."

"Like what?"

"I don't know. A note? Or a pouch?"

Willy bobbed his head and flew away.

"You should go. I'll meet you downstairs in the dining room."

"What?" Ben drew his attention from the window. "Oh, yeah. Right. I'll see you down there."

He took one last look at where Willy had been, shook his head in disbelief, and then departed.

When she was sure he was gone for good, Birdie slipped out of bed and went into the bathroom to wash up. She tugged on a fresh pair of shorts, then picked up the jeans she'd been wearing the night before. As she cleaned out the pockets, she found the aventurine.

She cupped it in her hand.

The golden knight still shimmered there. She rubbed at it with her thumb, but the image remained.

She slipped it into her pocket and left the room.

The Begijnhof, now the home of Benedictine nuns,
was a safe place in the Middle Ages for upper-class
unmarried or widowed women who wanted to dedicate
their time to charitable works. Known as beguines, they were
religious women who lived together in communities like the
Begijnhof, but were free to leave the order at any time.
Today, their simple white bungalows and red brick church still
surround a peaceful courtyard, which you are free to visit.

—*Marty McEntire,* Europe for Americans Travel Guide

CHAPTER TWENTY-SEVEN

When Birdie came downstairs, Ben was already at the table, looking miserable. His uncle and her mom were there, too, along with a family of four she'd never seen before. The mom and dad were sitting where Helga and Harry usually sat, which, for some reason, she found quite irritating.

Birdie slid into her seat beside Ben and picked up an airy croissant from the serving tray in the center of the table.

"Morning," she said.

"Good morning, Birdie." Uncle Noah had combed his shaggy hair this morning, and he was wearing a short-sleeved button-down oxford in place of his usual black T-shirt.

Before she could respond, Mrs. Devon whisked through the door.

"Good morning, everyone." She bustled between them with a carafe of coffee in one hand and a kettle of hot water in the other. "And you must be the Hammersmiths. Welcome to t'Bruges Huis."

The dark-haired father beamed at Mrs. Devon and introduced himself as Mark, then introduced his wife, Nancy, who sported a blond bob cut razor sharp just below her ears, and their two sons, Nick and Nelson. The boys shared their mother's blond hair and wore crisp-collared polo shirts. They were from Nebraska, Mark explained, and this was their first stop on the Continent after a brief stay in London. They were following the Marty McEntire Great Tour of Europe itinerary.

Uncle Noah and Mrs. Blessing introduced themselves and Ben and Birdie.

"This place is way better than the place we stayed in London." Nick waved his fork to emphasize his point. Birdie put him at about ten. "That was a plain Jane hotel. This place has style." He used the fork to stab a boysenberry pastry from the top tier of the tray.

Nelson, the younger of the two, rolled his eyes.

"Well, I am glad you approve," Mrs. Devon said, and then explained the breakfast options. Nick nodded appreciatively and ordered a three-egg omelet. When Mrs. Devon slipped back into the kitchen, Nick said to no one in particular, "See? Classy."

Ben tapped Birdie's foot under the table with his skateboarding sneaker. She gulped down a giggle as he grinned broadly beside her.

"Don't forget that we're going to the Church of Our Lady this morning," her mom said after the Hammersmiths settled into their own conversation and Birdie had regained her composure. "And then we'll need to pack up and get on the road."

"You're leaving already?" Nick said. "But we just got here."

"Well, we didn't," Birdie said. "We've been here a few days."

Nick slumped back in his chair.

Ben took his chance. "Mrs. Blessing, Uncle Noah?"

The adults exchanged glances across the table.

"Yes?" Uncle Noah set his coffee cup down and gave Ben his full attention.

"I know Mrs. Blessing wants to go to the church this morning, but do you think it would be okay if Birdie and I went on a bike ride after she gets all her stuff packed? She told me about the one she and her mom took and it sounded awesome."

"I don't know if there will be enough time," Mrs. Blessing said.

"I was thinking maybe we could go while you were studying the Michelangelo statue."

"Ben." Uncle Noah's jaw tightened.

"I just thought since they're leaving—"

"That you'd change their whole itinerary?"

"It's fine by me," Mrs. Blessing said with a sigh.

"Really?" Uncle Noah raised his eyebrows. "After…"

She nodded. "If it's okay with you."

He sat back in his seat, motioning for Mrs. Blessing to take the lead. She pulled her purse onto her lap, peeled a few bills from a roll of euros, and handed them to Birdie. "Just don't be late."

"Thanks, Mom."

"Wait. Here's the map."

"It's okay. You keep it. We know where the bike rental is and they have maps there if we need them."

Her mom slipped the worn map into her purse, closing the zippers tightly and latching the small set of hooks that held them closed against the prying fingers of experienced pickpockets. "Let's plan to meet back here at one o'clock. Then we can grab our bags, pick up some lunch, and head to the car rental place."

"Uncle Noah?"

He shook his head like he couldn't believe what he was about to say. "Sure, yes. Go ahead. I'll meet you back here at one."

Birdie and Ben exchanged glances and stood up. She tossed her napkin onto the table.

"We're going then," she said. "Since we don't have much time."

Ben snagged a large pastry from the top of the tray.

"You heard Mrs. Blessing," Uncle Noah said. "Do not be late."

"Got it. We won't," he said.

They said goodbye to the Hammersmiths and then slipped out through the sitting room. When they reached the foyer, Kayla swung down the steps and stepped between them.

"And where are we off to this fine morning?" She wore faded jean shorts and a loose-fitting tank top with peach-colored flowers on it. A pair of strappy leather sandals barely covered her feet.

"We?" Ben asked.

"Of course." Kayla gave them a sugary smile. "After that

card game last night, I thought it'd be fun to hang out with you two losers today."

"Come on," Birdie said, concerned that if they stayed in the foyer too long, her mom, or worse, Uncle Noah, would change their minds. She opened the door and held it for Ben and Kayla.

"So, where are we going?" Kayla asked after the door closed behind them.

"We're retracing our steps from last night. You'll need to keep up if you want to hang with us. We don't have much time." Ben started off at a fast clip toward the alley.

"Do you really think this is a good idea?" Kayla asked as she caught up to him.

Neither Birdie nor Ben answered as they zig-zagged through the lanes that led to the Begijnhof.

"Which way?" Ben said.

They'd reached the intersection where Henri and Marguerite had run from the boys. Birdie led them past the houses that had loomed so dark the night before. A few minutes later, they arrived at the stone bridge.

"There." She pointed to the park and the gate beyond. Other than swans and ducks, it was deserted this early in the morning. "That's where we went."

"The Minnewater?" Kayla asked.

"Follow me." Ben entered the park and passed the tree where they'd found the book.

"This is the Begijnhof," Kayla said as they cut across the courtyard with the tall grass and ancient trees. "The beguines live in those bungalows, or at least they used to. Now the Benedictine nuns live there. And that's their church. My grandparents dragged me out of bed to come over here the other morning."

When they reached the gate on the far end of the courtyard, it was closed and locked. Birdie glanced around, searching for another way through.

Kayla pulled out her phone. "Nine-fifteen. They don't open that gate for tourists until nine-thirty."

"Then why was the other gate open?" She pointed to the one they had just crossed through. "And they were both wide open last night."

"I don't know," Kayla said. "It probably has something to do with the church."

The bell in the steeple tolled once.

Kayla wandered toward the towering archway that led into the church.

"What are you doing?" Ben asked.

"It's a service. I'm going in." She stopped and looked at Ben and Birdie. "There's no way to get through that gate for another fifteen minutes and unless you know another way past it, I'd rather sit on a chair in the cool air of the church than bake out here in the sun."

Birdie checked her watch. "Okay," she said. "But not a minute longer."

The soaring sanctuary was dim and smoky, as if someone had blown the candles out and trapped the soot inside. Straight-backed wooden chairs, rather than pews, lined three sections. The main sanctuary faced the most prominent altar, with two smaller chapels flanking each side. The service was already underway and the priest's recitation reached them without the help of amplification.

Kayla moved across the tiled floor to the farthest chapel. She sat in the front row, and Birdie and Ben filed in beside her. A tray of candles of different sizes and in various stages of melting threw a warm glow on their skin.

"They're prayers," Kayla whispered. "You buy a candle and light it for your prayer. Usually they're in honor or memory of people."

"How do you know?" Birdie asked.

"Grammy and Gramps love going to churches. Grammy lights a candle in memory of each of the dogs they've had."

"Really?"

Kayla nodded.

"Consolation," Ben whispered.

"What?" Birdie asked.

"That's what this chapel is called. The Chapel of Consolation." He was reading a leaflet that someone had placed on the chairs.

Birdie found hers and turned to the section with the English translation.

"To bring peace to those who are lost, and console those who mourn," she read.

In front of them, a statue of the Virgin Mary holding Baby Jesus sat among flowers and greens.

Birdie closed her eyes and bowed her head.

She breathed in the still air, heavy with the fragrance of candle wax and incense. In the main sanctuary, the organist played the first note of a hymn, and the sisters began to sing.

She couldn't understand the words, but she recognized the ritual, the repetition, the cadence of the hymns. She allowed thoughts of Jonah and her father to come, to sit with her on her slender wooden chair at the altar of consolation.

This time, she didn't push them away.

The last time she'd been at a church service, it had been their funeral. She'd walked behind their caskets as they were taken to be buried together on the hill in the town cemetery.

Now they would be there forever.

"We all have to die sometime, Birdie."

Birdie's eyes fluttered open. She peeked at Kayla, then at Ben. They were both staring off into the church, lost in their own thoughts.

She looked up at the statue of the Virgin Mary.

It was just marble and wood.

Had she really heard something? Or was it her imagination, a trick of the light and the candles and the centuries-old chapel?

The music swelled, filling the sanctuary as the service ended.

The bell in the steeple tolled.

"It's time," Ben whispered.

Kayla nodded. "The gate should be opening. Let's go."

"Wait," Birdie said. "Hold on a second."

She dug in her pocket for the money her mother had given her for the bike, then stood and approached the tray of burning candles. A spiral stand next to the tray held the largest candles of all. They were in glass jars nearly eight inches tall and looked as if they would burn for days. Each one cost five euros.

Birdie folded the bill and pushed it into the slit on the top of the metal offering box, then selected a tall white candle.

She used a piece of wick to light it, then placed it on the very top rung of the spiral holder.

She watched it burn for a moment.

"Time to go," Kayla said behind her.

Birdie inhaled deeply.

When she turned away from the candle, Ben was watching her.

"For my dad and my brother," she said.

Ben nodded and followed her from the church.

CHAPTER TWENTY-EIGHT

They merged in line with the other worshippers, shuffling from the deep shadows of the sanctuary out into the daylight. Birdie shielded her eyes and squinted to see that the iron gate now stood open.

"Let's do this," Ben said.

They passed through the gate, dodging a stream of tourists making their way into the Begijnhof, then ducked through the hedge on the far side of the park.

"These bushes look different than they did last night." Birdie brushed a few errant pine needles from her shoulders. "They're bigger. And pricklier."

A few moments later, after checking to make sure no one was watching, they passed under the stone arch and into the darkened stairwell.

Ben halted on the spiral stairs. "Hold."

Birdie slammed into his back as Kayla plowed into her.

"Ow!" Birdie cried as she instinctively steadied herself against the stone walls.

"Shh." Ben turned toward her in the dark.

"What is it?"

"I thought I heard something." He cracked the door open and eased through it.

"Oh, for goodness sakes." Kayla pushed past him, threw the door open wide, and flooded the chamber with white light.

Birdie blinked, ready to turn and run.

"Now we can see where we're going." Kayla held her phone up so the bright stream of her flashlight swept down the long corridor. "It's a bar."

Birdie blinked again.

"Yes!" Ben stepped deeper into the room and spread his arms wide. "It's the Monk Bar. Didn't I tell you last night? I could have sworn it was the place where Uncle Noah and I had dinner. They call it the Monk Bar because they only carry beer brewed by monks. I thought it was the same place because of the arches. I know there are a ton of old arches around here, but I spent so much time staring at these while Uncle Noah quizzed the bartender that I recognized the pattern of the stones."

There was no sign of the kids they'd seen the night before, no fire to warm the cold stone slabs. The arched alcoves cocooned tables and chairs instead of bedding and clothes, candles and children. A polished bar with a dozen high-backed stools lined the far wall, with just enough space for a bartender to maneuver behind it.

"Well, that's freaky." Birdie peered under one of the arches, half expecting to see a pile of rags and children, but there were only more tables and chairs.

They were alone. It was too early for the bar backs to be slicing lemons and limes or preparing for the afternoon rush. The smoky, sausage-scented air from the night before had been supplanted by a heavy combination of yesterday's beer and something less pleasant, like the steam from the sewer grates they passed from time to time above.

"This isn't what it looked like last night," Birdie explained to Kayla.

"Are you sure you weren't sleepwalking?" She swept the light around the empty bar.

"Both of us? Not likely."

"Maybe you were dreaming."

"Because Birdie and I are telepathically connected and would have the exact same dream about a place that apparently doesn't even exist," Ben said.

Kayla narrowed her gaze. "Then how do you explain the fact that this bar miraculously changed? Are you sure you had the right hedge?"

"Do you want to hang out with us or not?" He folded his arms against his chest. "If you do, then you might want to shut the hell up. We're trying to figure this out."

Kayla wound up to say something snarky, but then her shoulders sagged and she shook her head. "Fine. So then let me help. If this place didn't look like this last night, what did it look like?"

"It wasn't a bar, for starters," Birdie said. "It was an... an orphanage almost. But no adults. There were kids here. Lots of kids. And a girl named Eva. I talked to her. She's the one who said I had to return the book or else."

"Or else what?"

"I don't know." The skin on her arms crawled at the memory of Eva touching her. "It was really creepy, okay? I just wanted to get out of there and I didn't prolong it by asking a lot of questions."

She shoved her hands in her pockets. The aventurine was there, warm against her skin. She tumbled it nervously, then brought it out to look at it. The knight was still there.

"What is that?" Kayla snatched it from her.

"Hey! Give it back!"

"It's hot." She turned the aventurine over in her palm, then dropped it into Birdie's outstretched hand.

"It was in my pocket."

"Whatever," Kayla said, the aventurine forgotten. "So this isn't the same place you losers were last night. This is a bar and, unless we do want trouble, we'd better get out of here. I don't want to get arrested for trespassing."

Ben stepped deeper into the chamber. "Here, let me see that." He held out his hand for Kayla's phone.

She hesitated and then handed it to him. "Don't drop it."

He shined the flashlight into each alcove. When he reached the end of the corridor, he turned around, temporarily blinding them before angling the phone toward the floor.

"There's nothing here except tables and chairs," he said from across the room. "I just don't understand it. Sorry, Birdie."

A key scraped in the door lock behind the bar. Ben's eyes grew wide, and he sprinted back to them.

They rushed toward the door to the stairs as Ben clicked off the light on the phone and shoved it into Kayla's hand.

"What the… Did you drop…" Kayla's words fell away as she pivoted to face him.

Birdie's vision acclimated to the dim light, and she shifted to follow Kayla's gaze.

"You came back." Eva was at the far end of the chamber strolling toward them. She was dressed as she had been the night before, with her hair swept across her shoulder in a long plait.

No one moved.

"Who are you?" she asked, sizing up Kayla. "And where are your clothes?"

"I could ask you the same thing." Kayla tilted her chin, but Birdie thought her voice sounded shakier than normal.

"I am Eva." She turned to Ben and Birdie. "The book?"

"We're looking for Henri." Birdie took a step forward. "We want to see him first."

"He is not here."

"Where is he?"

Eva didn't respond.

"Then we'll be back with the book after we find him."

She laughed. "No. I will take the book now."

"I don't have it."

"I am aware of that." Eva moved closer to her.

Kayla stepped between them. "Now hold up there. Last I heard, that book doesn't belong to you."

Eva raised her voice and called out in an unfamiliar language. The boys who'd been playing dice the night before strode out of the alcoves and flanked her on either side.

The beefy one called Jan grinned at Birdie. Every instinct told her to run, but she held firm.

"I will ask again," Eva said. "The book."

No one replied.

Kayla planted her hands on her hips. "That would be a no. There is no way in hell we're giving you anything." She looked beyond Eva and the boys. "What is this place, anyway?"

Eva murmured something in that odd tongue. It wasn't the French or Dutch that Birdie was coming to recognize, even if she didn't understand it. This sounded older and very different.

Suddenly, Eva seized Kayla by the arm.

"Hey!" She tried to shake off the thinner girl's grip. "Let me go!"

The boys quickly encircled them as Jan captured Ben from behind by his arms and yanked him away.

Ben thrashed hard against him as several other boys ran to Jan's aid. Ben fought their grasp, but they outnumbered him and he couldn't break free.

Together they dragged him down the long corridor, past the alcoves flickering with candlelight. As Ben wrestled against them, Jan snagged the pocket of his cargo shorts and tore it straight down.

The book tumbled to the floor.

"Eva!" Rat Boy swept in and picked it up with a dirty hand.

She stopped her argument with Kayla long enough to look his way. When she did, he tossed the book to her.

She caught it easily and called out, "*Merci*, Joos," before turning back to Kayla. "As I said, the book belongs to me."

"No, it doesn't!" Ben shouted, struggling again as the

boys pulled him deeper into the chamber.

Birdie chased them down the corridor. "Get back here! Where do you think you're taking him? You got your stupid book. Now let him go!"

They acted as if she hadn't said a word.

She ran harder, the footfalls of her sneakered feet silent on the cobblestone floor.

Kayla and Eva shouted at each other behind her, their voices echoing through the cold stone arches.

Birdie caught up quickly and reached out with both hands to nab Joos by the scruff of his coat collar.

She yanked him back as hard as she could.

She'd caught him off-guard. He fell toward her and lost his grip on Ben.

She pivoted to avoid his fall and went after Jan as Ben regained his footing. She gripped Jan by his collar and pulled as she'd done to Joos, but he proved heavier and more powerful.

Maintaining his grip on Ben, Jan yelled something that Birdie didn't understand.

Several alcoves ahead of them, the boys who were leading the way turned around, then reversed course and charged at Ben. The tallest one punched him hard in the jaw while a stubby one grabbed his free arm and dragged him swiftly away. Ben kicked with his skateboarding sneakers but couldn't gain traction on the cobbled floor.

Birdie refused to release Jan, even as she struggled to hold on. "Let him go!" she screamed.

Strong hands circled her waist and pulled her backward, hard. Jan's collar slid from her grasp, and she found herself facedown on the floor, gasping for air.

She rolled over in time to see Joos laughing as he ran to catch up with the rest of the boys, who were dragging Ben through a doorway at the far end of the corridor. They shimmered as he approached.

"Ben!" she cried, but her voice sounded funny, even to herself, as if she were yelling through water.

She attempted to scramble to her feet, but her head throbbed and the best she could do was sit up.

Pinpoints of light floated into view and hung there. She rubbed her eyes, desperate to clear them away.

As her vision slowly returned she searched the corridor, but it was no use.

Ben was already gone.

CHAPTER TWENTY-NINE

"No." Birdie closed her eyes and rubbed the knot that was forming on her forehead where she'd knocked it against an uneven stone.

An alarm was screeching, piercing the air.

"Birdie, are you awake?" Kayla shook her shoulder. "We need to go. Now."

She opened her eyes and gasped.

They were back in the bar. The cobblestone floor now supported a maze of chair and table legs. Kayla's phone was once again throwing a bright circle of light around them.

"Someone's coming." Kayla nearly dropped her phone as she tried to kill the light.

As Birdie struggled to her feet, she heard a door sliding open behind the bar.

Kayla anchored an arm under her shoulder, and they started back toward the door by the stairs.

"Ben." Birdie glanced over her shoulder.

"He's not here." Kayla pulled her along.

The alarm ceased and the room flooded with light. They froze, stranded a few feet from the door that led to the spiral staircase and freedom.

A bar back danced in and flipped on more overhead lights. He was jamming to music on his headphones and hadn't noticed them. When he turned his back to grab something from behind the bar, they slipped out the door.

"Are you okay?" Kayla asked after they'd scrambled up the stairs and cleared the other side of the hedge.

Birdie collapsed on the damp grass. "Oh my God. Oh... my... God. Kayla. Ben is gone. They have Ben. What are we going to do? What are they going to do? Oh my God!"

"Birdie." Kayla's voice was stern. "Get a grip. We'll figure this out." She glanced around the park and then back at the hedge. "Whatever the hell this is."

"We need to find him," Birdie said.

"What about the book?"

"Who cares about the stupid book? We can't go back without Ben. We need to get back in there." She tried to stand up again, but Kayla touched her shoulder and sat down beside her.

"What we need is a plan," she said. "We need to think. Think first, then act."

"I think we need to go back in there and get Ben!"

"And I think we should try to find the kid you were talking about."

"They could hurt him. They probably are hurting him. What am I going to tell his uncle?" Her eyes grew wide and started to sting.

"Birdie. Concentrate. We need to find the kid who hid the

book. He's our best bet for getting Ben back. He'll know those kids, and he'll know his way around that dungeon. Now think." Kayla grabbed her shoulders and gave a firm shake. "Where would he be?"

"Henri?" Birdie swiped at the tears that were forming.

"Yes, right. Henri. What's been the common link when you saw Henri?"

Birdie's mind raced. What were they going to do to Ben? "Birdie?"

"I don't know." She shook her head.

Kayla gave her a hard look.

A fat tear escaped and slid down her cheek.

"We will never find Ben if you can't pull yourself together. Now quit crying and think."

"Okay, okay." She rubbed her face and then looked at Kayla. "He waves."

"Okay, that's good." She bared her teeth in an attempt at a smile. "He waves. He waves when you see him?"

"Yes. He always waves to us."

"Is there anything happening before you see him? Maybe something you haven't thought about? Are you always in the same place?"

Birdie stared at the water cascading through the fountain and tried to concentrate on the question.

"The first time I saw him, Ben and I were on the brewery roof. He was in the park and an old woman – a nun – was chasing him."

"Okay, good. What about the next time?"

Birdie explained her encounters with Henri on the canal cruise, in the alley by t'Bruges Huis, and on the street in front of his house.

"Wait, you know where he lives?" Kayla couldn't keep the excitement from her voice as she rocked up onto her knees. "Then let's go get him."

"No, he doesn't actually live there." She rubbed her eyes. "Well, I'm not sure if he lives there."

"Damn it, Birdie, do you know where he lives or not?"

"I saw him go into this house. His little sister was there too. Her name is Marguerite. She's adorable. But when Ben and I went there to find him, the only person home was Mrs. Winggen, and she swears there are no children in the house and there haven't been for years."

"Okay." Kayla's tone made it clear that she didn't really think Birdie was okay. "Let's see. What else might matter?" Her eyes lit up. "Did you always have the book with you when you saw him?"

"No."

"Did he always have the book?"

"No."

The light in her eyes dimmed. "Was Ben always with you?"

"Yes! No. Wait. He wasn't with me on the canal cruise. My mom was."

"What does Henri look like?"

"He looks… different." Birdie closed her eyes and pictured her drawing. "He wears thick pants that are kind of like tights, but they're too wide and too long at the same time. His feet are almost always bare and when they're not, he wears shoes that are too big for him and look kind of like moccasins. His shirt is white and I think it has hooks instead

214

of buttons. His hair is shaggy and sandy blond, and his eyes are green. He's shorter than me, but I think he's my age." She opened her eyes.

Kayla considered Birdie's answer as they sat together on the grass. A few more people had entered the park, but none of them seemed interested in Birdie and Kayla.

She glanced at the hedge, hoping against hope she'd see Ben coming through it.

But there was no one there.

"I don't know what to think. From what you described, it's like he's from another time, or maybe a reenactor? And that creepy dungeon? I don't even know what to assume about that place. And how did it change?"

"What did you say?" Birdie sat up straighter.

"The creepy dungeon..."

"No, before that."

"I said I thought it sounded like Henri was from a different time."

Birdie got to her feet. "That's it. Of course!"

"What's it?"

"Why didn't we see it before? That explains everything. The flowers, the book, why Henri kept disappearing, everything!" She reached into her pocket. "That's how we can find Henri. That's how we can get back to Ben."

"What are you talking about?"

"The aventurine." She pulled the cinnamon-colored oval from her pocket and held it in her palm.

"That little stone? How?"

"It's glass. Venetian glass. I'm not sure. I don't understand how it works." She pondered the legend they'd read in the brewery gift shop. "I'm not sure I'm supposed to understand. But it led Ben and me to the book, so maybe it will lead us to Henri."

As she spoke, the knight slowly dissolved, and the gold sparkles swirled.

She rubbed the aventurine, and they swirled faster. When the glass grew too hot to hold, she dropped it on the grass between them.

"What's it doing?" Kayla stared at the beautiful glass.

"Just watch."

The gold shimmered and swirled. It seemed to take forever to decide on a shape, but when it did, all the gold flew into the coppery center.

"What is it?"

"A bear." Birdie bent closer to examine the image. "And I've seen it before. Somewhere here in Bruges."

"I know where!" Kayla jumped up and swept the dirt from her bare legs. "It hangs outside t'Bruges Huis. On the sign that swings out front."

"You're right. Come on!"

They sprinted through the narrow streets, skirting tour groups and ticket lines. When they reached the lane, Kayla stopped. They were still a few houses away from t'Bruges Huis.

"Hold on," she panted, bending to rest her hands on her knees.

Birdie left her there and approached the wood and metal sign that swayed out front.

There it was, a coat of arms with a standing bear in the

middle, holding a letter B.

Please let Ben be inside. Maybe he'd made it back somehow.

Or Henri. Maybe Henri was here, inside with Marguerite, waiting for them in the sitting room.

She pulled the aventurine from her pocket and held it up. No.

It couldn't be.

"See," Kayla said, reaching her side, still out of breath. "There it is."

"No, it isn't." Birdie thrust the aventurine under Kayla's nose. "It's not the same. The bear is different. The one on the glass doesn't have a B on it."

"It's so close, though." Kayla studied the two images.

Birdie rubbed the aventurine, but the standing bear held fast.

"Let's go inside, anyway." Kayla leaned against the wall of the house next door. "Maybe it's close enough. The symbol could have changed with time."

They started toward the front door, but Birdie stopped and held her finger to her lips to silence Kayla. She pointed to the front windows of t'Bruges Huis. They were tilted open to let the cool breeze pass through the house. Voices floated out to them from inside.

"So you're telling me they came to your house?" It was Uncle Noah. As usual, he did not sound happy. "When was this?"

"Yesterday, in the afternoon." There was no mistaking Mrs. Winggen's Tinker Bell voice. "We had a lovely tea together. They're quite well-behaved children. You should be proud of yourselves. Oh thank you, dear."

"You're welcome, Mrs. Winggen," Mrs. Devon said. Birdie wondered what she was doing there so late in the morning.

"Yes, thank you," her mom repeated.

"Be sure to let me know if you need anything else," Mrs. Devon said.

Birdie recognized the sound of a teacup joining its saucer. She didn't dare pop onto her tiptoes to peer in the window. They crouched low beneath the ledge.

"Why weren't they with you?" Uncle Noah asked.

Her mom didn't answer him and instead asked, "Why did they come to see you?"

"It was the strangest thing," Mrs. Winggen said. "They were looking for another boy. I told them no boys had lived in the house for ages, of course."

Mrs. Winggen continued for several minutes, explaining the home's lineage and talking about her daughters.

Kayla threw a questioning look at Birdie, who held her finger up. "Just wait," she mouthed.

Mrs. Blessing gently steered the older woman back to the matter at hand. "Was that all Ben and Birdie wanted, Mrs. Winggen? To see if the boy lived at your house?"

No one said anything for a long time. Birdie could hear the porcelain cups and saucers clinking. Then Mrs. Winggen spoke.

"They had a book with them. An old, leather-bound book."

"Yes, I've seen them looking at something like that," Mrs. Blessing said.

"You have?" Uncle Noah asked.

"You didn't notice the giant bulge weighing down the side of Ben's shorts all week?"

Mrs. Winggen continued as if she hadn't heard them. "You see, after they left, I climbed up to the attic and pulled out an old family ledger. I'd nearly forgotten it was there. I don't climb those stairs very often now with the arthritis in my knees. The doctor says…"

Mrs. Blessing cleared her throat.

"Oh, yes, right. Well, the ledger was up there. It's one of those things that belongs to the house, if you can understand that. It will stay with it as long as the house stands. It's quite heavy and—"

"What did you find in the ledger?" Uncle Noah asked.

"Yes, it was quite interesting. It turns out there was a gentleman named Henri LeFort who lived in the house. He claimed it in 1515. Few people had much use for Bruges by then. The town's time had passed." There was a pause, then Birdie heard the cup clink with the saucer again.

"Let's see. He would have been my great-grandfather many times over. The Witte Beertje Huis – our houses had names then, you see, it was long before they thought to give them numbers. In English it means White Bear House. Yes, so Witte Beertje Huis had been vacant for more than a decade by the time Henri came to Bruges with his sister, Marguerite. I imagine it was in a sorry state. Why he would want it, I don't know, but he claimed he had a right to it.

"There are notes in the ledger, the handwriting is tiny and neat, that say the aldermen didn't believe him at first. He and Marguerite had been listed in the town archives as being sent to France to live with an uncle after their parents died, with a note that they'd never arrived. They were presumed dead, of course, two children alone in the world. How horrible it must have been for them. You would think some of the aldermen would have noticed Henri's resemblance to his father since his father had been an alderman himself. But they didn't, I suppose. So much had changed by then. So many people had died and so many had abandoned the town. There was so much violence here after the ships stopped coming to Bruges."

Birdie heard the cup clink against the saucer again.

"In the end there was no proof it wasn't his family's house," Mrs. Winggen continued, "and because it had been vacant for so long, the aldermen waived their argument. An occupied house meant taxes in the coffers, you see. My family has lived in Witte Beertje Huis ever since."

Mrs. Winggen began to talk about her mother and father.

Birdie motioned to Kayla, and they scooted out from under the ledge.

"Now what?" Kayla whispered.

"I have an idea. Come on!" Birdie sprinted toward the alley.

You'll see coats of arms all over Bruges –
on public buildings, on private houses, even in the churches.
The families of the merchants were very important to the town,
and each family had its own coat of arms. They were positioned
in different places around Bruges in their honor, and
to remind people who was in charge.

—*Marty McEntire,* Europe for Americans Travel Guide

CHAPTER THIRTY

"Where are we going?" Kayla asked several minutes later as they slowed to weave across a crowded bridge.

"Henri's house."

"I thought you said he doesn't really live there?"

"Just… come on."

"Remind me to wear different shoes next time I decide to go out with you." Kayla adjusted the straps on her kitten-heel sandals. Angry blisters were forming beneath the thin leather.

They continued along the canal until they reached the spot where Henri's house sat. Birdie pulled the aventurine from her pocket and it grew hot.

"Look." She nodded toward the house where Henri lived.

The flowers were red and purple again.

"It's the bear!" Kayla pointed to the window boxes. A coat of arms with a bear standing proudly peeked out from beneath the blooms.

Birdie held up the aventurine. The images matched.

"You're right!"

She sprinted to the front door, with Kayla close behind her. She pulled the long iron bell and listened as its chime echoed inside.

Quick steps approached, a peephole slid open, and then the latch clicked. Birdie stepped into the vestibule, with Kayla on her heels.

"Henri," Birdie said as the door closed behind them. He eyed Kayla cautiously. "She's my... friend," Birdie said, trying for a smile but failing.

Henri led them through the interior door and into the foyer. Light shone through the stained glass windows and created a lovely pattern on the wooden floor, just as it had the day before when she and Ben had tea with Mrs. Winggen.

But today the house was different. The air inside was laden with dust, creosote, and age. Rays of sun flooded the parlor, picking up the layers of soot that hung in the air. Hulking furniture hid beneath heavy sheets.

Henri stood beside them in the foyer, while Marguerite sat on the parlor's bare floor near an anemic flame that flickered behind the fireplace grate. Despite the spring-like weather outside, it felt cold and damp within the thick walls of the medieval home.

"Mon livre?"

"I... we don't have it anymore," Birdie said, understanding the French words for my book after hearing them so many times. "We need your help to get it back."

"Back?"

Birdie nodded. "From Eva. Eva took it from Ben. Her

gang of boys did it."

Henri's green eyes grew wide and fear flickered across them.

Birdie's stomach sank. "Are they the same boys who chased you the other night?"

"*Non.*" Henri shook his head. "Worse. That is why I went to the…" He paused, searching for the English word. "Cave. *La cave à vin.* Wine."

Henri waved away the confusion that must have crossed Birdie's face and added, "They are loyal to Eva."

"Are you loyal to Eva?"

"*Non!*" He grew agitated. "Never to Eva."

"But she protected you. From those boys."

Henri scowled. "I pay for Eva's protection. But never with my father's book. We must get it back. Where did they take it?"

As Birdie explained what happened, speaking each word slowly to make sure Henri understood, Kayla moved into the parlor and lowered herself to the floor beside Marguerite.

"Hello," Kayla said, her voice soft and light.

Marguerite's eyes darted to Henri.

He nodded.

"*Hallo,*" she whispered.

Kayla traced her finger in the dust. "My name is Kayla."

"Marguerite."

"That's a pretty name."

Birdie didn't know if Marguerite understood the compliment, but she rewarded Kayla with a wisp of a smile. Her petite face looked more childlike at that moment than it had at any other time Birdie had seen her.

Kayla drew a circle on the floor with her finger and added big, round eyes. She glanced at Marguerite expectantly.

Marguerite placed a tiny finger in the dust and drew the curve of a smiling mouth.

Kayla added a nose.

Marguerite studied the face and added sweeps of long hair. It would be a girl.

"Ben is gone? You do not know where?" Henri asked.

She pulled her gaze from the girls. "He was in the dungeon... the cave. That's the last place we saw him."

"We must go," Henri said. "The boys are dangerous."

"But what will we do?"

Henri walked into the parlor and tugged on a heavy sheet. It shifted just a little, revealing a beautiful bureau. He opened the top drawer and retrieved something small, which he dropped into his pocket before covering the elegant piece of furniture again.

"We must go," he repeated, then addressed Marguerite in French.

She stood, the hem of her skirt falling to her ankles, and offered a tiny hand to Kayla.

Kayla laced her fingers with Marguerite's and stood. They followed Henri and Birdie back out onto the street.

Kayla gasped.

The cobblestone lane was empty, except for a pair of horses drawing an over-full wagon a block away. A string of barges weighed down with goods crawled through the canal as the scents of sea and smoke laced into an unlikely perfume.

Henri bowed his head and hugged the facades of the buildings as they passed, trying to make himself as inconspicuous as possible. Birdie remained close as they entered the park and then passed through the gate into the Begijnhof courtyard.

"*Tu! Garçon!*"

The aged voice cracked as if coming to them through ancient stereo speakers. Birdie sought the source of the words and discovered a petite woman in heavy black robes.

Henri shouted, "*Cours!* Run!"

Birdie and Kayla took off after Henri at a fast clip, skirting the tall trees in the courtyard and passing through the gate on the other end. They sprinted across the grass, through the opening in the hedge, and down the narrow dirt path before ducking under the archway.

"That was the nun from the park—the one we thought you stole the book from," Birdie gasped when they reached the door at the bottom of the spiral stairs. Kayla pulled up behind her, panting. Marguerite stayed tucked up beside the older girl.

"Stole?" Henri's quiet voice sounded incredulous. "It is my book. *Mon père…* My father bought that book. It is that beguine who wants to steal it from me!"

"The beguine? You mean the nun? But why?" Birdie asked.

"For gold. Monsieur Caxton is gone to England and his books are rare. My parents… they are gone. The aldermen ordered the beguines to care for us until they found our *maman's* family in France. *Non.* The beguines will steal all we have left."

"How do you know?"

Henri didn't answer.

"Will you go to France?"

"*Non. Maman's* family is *la morte*, dead. The plague took them too."

"What will you do?"

"Marguerite and I will leave Bruges with all we can carry as soon as we can make safe passage."

"To where?"

"Shhh." Henri held up his hand. He pressed his ear to the door, listened closely, then turned to Birdie.

"He is alive."

"You can hear him?"

"*Oui.*"

Birdie's pulse quickened. "Does he sound okay?"

"He is playing a game. Cards."

"Cards?" Kayla asked. "Seriously?"

Henri pushed the door open and they entered the chamber in silence, easing the door closed behind them.

Under the stone arches at the end of the long corridor, the boys Birdie tried to fight off were sitting in a circle on the floor. Henri was right. They were playing cards.

Ben was with them, his eye bruised and swollen, his arms bound behind his back. His bottom lip was fat and decorated by a trail of dried blood leading down his chin. He gestured as well as he could with his chin and said, "Now you want to lay down this one."

He repeated the sentence in French and Jan dropped a card on the pile with sausage-like fingers.

Birdie felt movement behind her and watched, unable to say a word without drawing attention to herself, as Marguerite led Kayla away down a narrow side hall toward the alcoves. She met her gaze as they passed and Kayla gave her a thumbs-up.

Henri and Birdie stared in silence as the card game unfolded, Ben instructing Jan and a younger boy he called Jacob on their moves.

The lump on Birdie's head throbbed at the sight of them.

"Regard!" Henri cried suddenly.

Birdie flinched and nearly screamed. Before she could see where he was pointing, a snarling voice rose behind them.

"Look who's back."

Birdie spun and found herself face to face with the rat-faced teenager, Joos, his long hair pooling on his shoulders, and his teeth dark and crooked behind thin, scarred lips. She could hear the other boys getting to their feet.

Henri addressed Joos in Dutch. Birdie didn't know what he was saying, but even from across the room she could tell that Ben was listening intently. She wondered if he understood Dutch as well as he did French.

After a moment's conversation, Henri pulled out the item he'd retrieved from the bureau drawer. To Birdie's amazement, it was a sparkling green jewel the size of a pencil eraser.

Joos eyed the jewel, then snatched it from Henri's palm. He placed it between his teeth and bit down. When nothing happened, he pulled it from his mouth and nodded at Henri, murmuring something that sounded appreciative. Then he strolled away toward the card game. When Birdie and Henri fell into step behind him, he wheeled around and struck.

Birdie dodged his fist and landed the hardest kick she could to his kneecap. Her sneakers softened the blow, but it was enough to knock him off balance. As he stumbled, Henri pushed him hard.

Joos yelled, and the other boys abandoned the card game. Everything happened quickly then.

The jewel tumbled from Joos's hand and Henri scooped it up. Behind them, a girl's scream filled the corridor, followed by a heavy thud. Birdie didn't dare take her eyes off the pack of boys bearing down on them. Ben, forgotten in the commotion, struggled to his feet. His arms were still secured behind his back, but he sprinted toward them on long legs.

There was movement all around them then, as Birdie and Henri each ducked and she swung her leg to trip Jan and Jacob. A moment later, Ben was by her side.

As the boys scrambled to their feet, Ben, Birdie, and Henri ran toward the door.

CHAPTER THIRTY-ONE

Henri threw the door open, and they flew up the spiral staircase. A moment later, they passed through the archway and were blinded by sunlight. They ducked under the hedge and kept going, putting space between them and the chamber.

They sprinted across the courtyard and through the iron gate, weaving through the stands of windswept trees. They'd almost cleared them when a woman stepped out from behind a tree and snagged Henri by the collar, yanking him backward and nearly off his feet.

"Le livre," she demanded.

Ben and Birdie slowed, stopped, and spun around.

The beguine was slight, no more than five feet tall, dressed in long black robes with thick white scarves that cupped her face and neck. A black hood stood out firmly on each side to conceal her head, as if there were a small umbrella inside propping it up.

In the distance, the boys exploded out from behind the

hedge with Eva at their side. Her cheek was split and blood dripped down her face. When they saw the beguine holding Henri, they reared back, retreating toward the dungeon in slow motion.

Birdie rushed to untie Ben.

Meanwhile, the beguine was turning out Henri's pockets.

"Non, Madame, s'il vous plaît!" he protested, twisting in her grasp.

Birdie saw a flash of green as the jewel in Henri's pocket broke loose from the fabric and tumbled to the ground. He shifted his foot to cover it.

The beguine delivered a warning and then let him go with a rough push. Henri stumbled but held his footing. She said something else to him, and he bowed deeply.

The beguine turned aside, but did not rush to leave. She glided away from Henri, who stood rooted to the spot. He stayed there until she reached the garden gate that led to her whitewashed bungalow and disappeared behind it.

"What was that all about?" Ben asked after Henri scooped up the jewel and ran to catch up.

"Où est Marguerite?" He searched the courtyard. "Where is my sister?"

"She was with Kayla." Birdie took a step toward the dungeon. "We need to—"

"No." Ben stuck his arm out to block the way. "If you're fixing to go back in that place, you can forget it right now."

The concern on his battered face stopped her in her tracks.

"Marguerite knows where to hide." Henri stared toward the dungeon, hesitating a moment before walking again.

"She knows where to meet me."

"You're just going to leave her there?" Birdie opened her hands wide.

Henri looked at the ground. "It is the only way for now."

"What about Kayla?"

"Marguerite will see her safe."

Ben and Birdie exchanged glances.

Two more beguines emerged from one of the bungalows and began gliding toward them.

"We must go," Henri said, urgency filling his voice as he motioned for Birdie and Ben to follow him. "They know me."

They made their way swiftly from the park, following the canal back to the house with the red and purple flowers.

They followed Henri onto the front stoop and watched anxiously as he fitted an old key in the large lock. It twisted several times and then clicked. He pushed the door open and led them into the foyer, greeted by the now familiar fragrance of dust and wood smoke.

"*Merci. Merci beaucoup.* Thank you," Ben said. "Thank you for coming back. I don't know how I would have got out of there otherwise."

"With your card-playing skills, it looked like," Birdie said as she examined a small tear near the hem of her shirt.

Ben laughed, but there was no humor in it. "I was teaching them to play. I was buying time. It made me useful."

"Thank goodness for those French classes."

"Yeah. If my parents only knew." He turned to Henri. "*Désolé.* I'm sorry. I lost your book."

Henri was about to answer when a pleasant voice startled them from the sitting room.

"Do you mean this book?"

Birdie turned to see Kayla and Marguerite resting in a soft patch of sunlight in front of the fireplace, working on their dust masterpieces. She held the leather volume up with her free hand.

Marguerite grinned.

"Kayla!" Birdie ran into the room. "You got out!"

"Yes, I did." She smiled. "With Marguerite's help, of course."

"How did you get the book?" Ben didn't bother to hide his surprise as he followed Birdie into the room.

"Hmmm." Kayla exchanged a knowing glance with Marguerite. "Let's just say I encouraged Eva to hand it over."

She held up her bloodstained knuckles.

"That's awesome!" Ben's crooked smile lit up his battered face.

"I couldn't have managed it without Marguerite, though."

The little girl leaned into Kayla for a quick hug.

"Well, it is done then," Henri said, letting out a tired breath.

They were all quiet for a moment.

"What will you do now?" Birdie asked.

Henri made his way across the room. He stopped beside Marguerite.

"We will leave Bruges. Soon."

He looked past the lace sheers to the canal beyond, as if

he were planning his route.

"Very soon. As soon as it is safe. I have my father's maps. He has friends in Venice. He told me to take Marguerite there if anything ever happened to *Maman*."

Marguerite stared at her drawing on the dusty floor.

"That is a long journey," Ben said.

"*Oui,*" Henri agreed. "But we are prepared."

"I guess you'll be needing this," Kayla said, holding the book out to him.

He reached for it.

As his fingers grasped the corner of the leather-bound book, a taxi horn blared just outside the window.

"What the hell?" Ben said, as Birdie let out a small yelp. Kayla jumped too.

The taxi had startled them all.

Except for Henri and Marguerite.

They were gone.

"Birdie…" Kayla began, but seemed unable to continue.

The room around them had changed. Instead of dusty floors and sheet-covered furniture, a lovely storyteller carpet fanned out beneath a love seat and two armchairs. A porcelain tea set sat on a low coffee table between them.

"Whaaa?" Kayla regained her voice. Behind her, the plain brick mantle was now a carved work of art. "What the hell just happened?"

Ben chuckled, and Birdie burst out laughing.

"We did it," he said, holding up his hand to high-five Birdie.

She smacked her hand against his. "We sure did. Now let's get out of here before Mrs. Winggen comes home."

Birdie helped Kayla up. "Thank you for getting the book. I'm glad you came today. We couldn't have done this without you."

"No problem." She averted her eyes.

Birdie thought they might have been filling with tears.

Kayla swiped at the back of her dusty shorts, then stared at the spot where Marguerite had drawn pictures with her only moments before. "I'm gonna miss that kid."

"She will never forget you," Birdie said. "I'm sure of it."

"We need to go." Ben scanned the street through the large window, then headed toward the foyer. "The last thing we need is to get caught here."

Birdie checked to make sure nothing looked out of place.

"Birdie, come on." He was already standing by the front door with Kayla.

"Okay, okay, I was just…" She stepped into the foyer. "Ben. Look."

There, in the center of the antique accent table, lay a leather-bound book with a faded knight embossed on its worn cover.

Kayla walked over to the table. "He forgot—"

"No," Birdie said. She gently opened the cover and saw the ancient handwritten script on the brittle paper. "He remembered."

*Before you leave Bruges, take one last stroll around
its peaceful back streets and imagine what it must
have been like to live here during its golden age.*

—*Marty McEntire*, Europe for Americans Travel Guide

CHAPTER THIRTY-TWO

Birdie, Ben, and Kayla made sure the heavy front door at Witte Beertje Huis was closed tight and locked behind them.

The morning mist had cleared, making way for a beautiful afternoon. A fresh batch of tourists meandered along the cobblestone lanes, pausing to photograph the sparkling canal, the colorful stepping-stone roofs, and the towering Gothic spires.

A warm breeze lifted the dark hair from Birdie's shoulders as they walked silently through the crowd. Every so often, someone would point at them, but no one said a thing.

They followed the sweep of the lane that bordered the canal, and then, for the last time, turned down the alley that would lead them to t'Bruges Huis and back to their normal, ordinary lives.

Above them, a chorus of wood pigeons called to one another as they rustled from rooftop to rooftop of the tightly packed houses.

When they neared the front door of t'Bruges Huis, Birdie checked the time.

12:55 pm.

She held her wrist up to show Ben and Kayla the face of her watch.

They were on time. She couldn't believe it. After everything that happened that morning, it was a miracle they weren't late.

They made their way up the wide steps to the front door, the three of them side by side. Birdie punched in the code on the green pad, and the door buzzed, then clicked open. Ben held it, then followed them into the foyer.

As the door latched behind them, the out-of-tune bells at the nearby church tolled.

"What in holy hell happened to you?" boomed Uncle Noah, bolting up from the armchair he'd been sitting in. Kayla's grandparents were on the love seat, and Birdie's mom was in the other chair.

They'd pulled a third armchair from the foyer for Mrs. Winggen. Birdie had completely forgotten she was there.

Ben's swollen, blood-streaked face twisted in surprise at his uncle's reaction. Then Birdie saw understanding creep into his deep brown eyes. He turned to examine himself in the foyer mirror.

He grinned and his features contorted like a mask. He touched a thin cut under his eye where they'd punched him. Trickles of dried blood crusted his face, and the ripped pocket of his shorts hung limp against his leg.

"Guess I should have cleaned myself up," he said

sheepishly.

"Yes, you probably should have." Uncle Noah placed his hands on his nephew's shoulders and stood behind him, so they both reflected in the mirror. Ben winced. Birdie had a feeling he had a bruise or two on his shoulders too.

"So I'll ask you again. What the hell happened? Did you wreck the bikes?" He glanced at Birdie and Kayla's reflections in the mirror. "Into each other?"

Ben shook his head.

Mrs. Blessing had reached Birdie by then and cupped her face gently in her hands. "Are you okay? Where have you been? Is that a… bruise on your forehead?" She brushed her cool fingers along the lump. Birdie flinched.

"Kayla?" Harry said as he and Helga shuffled into the foyer. "What's the meaning of all this? You're filthy. Do we need to call the police?"

"Did that boy do this to you?" her mom asked. "The one you were searching for?"

"I sure hope the other guy looks worse." Uncle Noah eyed Ben's face.

"They do," Birdie said.

Everyone shifted to stare at her.

"They?" her mom repeated.

There were several beats of silence before Kayla stepped in. "Ben and Birdie got into a tussle with some kids who were trying to steal that boy's book."

"Ah ha. So you found him then," came a lilting voice from the parlor.

Birdie disengaged herself from her mom and approached Mrs. Winggen. Ben and Kayla followed her.

"We did, Mrs. Winggen." She lowered herself to the carpet beside the old woman's chair. Kayla and Ben sat down also. "His name was Henri. We found his little sister, Marguerite too."

Mrs. Winggen looked at them curiously with her deeply hooded eyes, sizing them up before she spoke.

"And the book?"

"Henri…" Birdie paused. "We returned it to Henri."

"It was safely in his hands? You are sure?"

"Yes, ma'am," Ben said.

"Very well." Mrs. Winggen supported her slight weight on the arms of the chair as she stood. "Then I suppose it is gone for good."

Ben, Birdie, and Kayla exchanged glances.

"I think it may turn up again," Birdie said.

Mrs. Winggen winked at her. "I think you may be right, dear."

"Mrs. Winggen was telling us she thought the book might be a family heirloom," Helga said. "It's been lost for many years."

"Yes." The old woman's face grew soft, as if she were collecting a memory from a faraway place. "I'd seen it only once, when I was a girl, and that was in the library of the old Begijnhof. I asked about it many years later, but the sisters said it disappeared. I'd forgotten all about it until you joined me for tea yesterday and showed me the book you found in the Minnewater. I couldn't be sure, of course, but I thought it might be the same book, a book about playing chess, a rare copy. But that wasn't why it was so special to my father.

"You see, tucked inside, sewn in with thick threads, were

the handwritten pages of a journal."

Ben and Birdie exchanged glances.

"According to my father, it belonged to my great-grandfather many times over, Henri LeFort. He'd written about a journey he took to Venice with his young sister and their time there. He'd followed in his dead father's footsteps and made a fortune as a merchant. He returned to Bruges as a young man and claimed his father's home. My home."

"Witte Beertje Huis," Birdie said.

Mrs. Winggen nodded.

"What a coincidence that the boy you met was also named Henri," Helga said.

"Yes," Mrs. Winggen agreed. "Quite a coincidence indeed." She ambled across the parlor to the foyer as the children got to their feet.

"The mystery is solved, and your children are home," Mrs. Winggen said, touching Mrs. Blessing's arm, and nodding to Uncle Noah, Helga, and Harry. "I shall take my leave. It was a pleasure to meet you all. I wish you safe travels. Please thank Mrs. Devon for the tea."

The adults said their farewells and stepped aside to let Mrs. Winggen pass. Uncle Noah opened the door for her and offered his elbow for support.

"Are you okay getting home?" he asked as they descended the steps. "I could call you a taxi."

"Yes, young man, I can manage. I have walked these lanes for eighty-three years." She paused to make sure he was listening. "And those taxi drivers are a nuisance. You'd do well to remember that."

"Yes, ma'am," he said. She slipped her hand from his

arm.

Uncle Noah watched until she turned up the alley, then came back into the foyer and closed the door.

All eyes turned to Birdie, Ben, and Kayla, who stood together as a motley crew in the sitting room.

"You should be punished for what you've been doing the past few days," Mrs. Blessing said.

Birdie started to protest, but Uncle Noah spoke first.

"I agree." He stepped forward until he stood next to Mrs. Blessing. Ben made a sound, but Uncle Noah held up his hand to silence him. "However, the Blessings are leaving this afternoon and we're staying in Belgium for a couple more days before we head to Berlin." He looked at Harry.

"We're leaving in the morning," he said, his white mustache wiggling as he spoke. He leveled his gaze at Kayla. "Bright and early."

"Okay, okay," she said. "I get it. I'll set the alarm on my phone." She patted the pocket of her jean shorts to make sure it was still there, but she didn't take it out.

"So," Uncle Noah continued, "your adventures together appear to be over."

Birdie lowered her head and stared at her sneakers to hide the tears that had leapt unbidden to her eyes. She didn't dare to look at Ben or Kayla.

"You all look exhausted," her mom said. "And you're filthy. Birdie, go upstairs and get yourself cleaned up, then grab your things. We need to be at the car rental shop in half an hour. We'll have to grab lunch on the road. Mrs. Devon has been more than gracious allowing us to keep the room so late on our check-out day."

Birdie stepped into the foyer, the mosaic floor reminding her of the stocky man who'd come to repair the tiny tiles in his ill-fitting clothes. There was no sign of his labor now, and she suspected it had been completed centuries ago. Ben followed her gaze, realization dawning in his eyes.

He motioned toward the stairs as the adults moved past them into the sitting room and spoke in low voices.

When they reached the first landing, Birdie stopped.

"I guess this is it," she said, breaking the silence that was building.

"I guess," Ben said.

"Where are you going next?" Kayla asked.

"I have no idea," Birdie said. Then she thought for a moment. "Germany, I guess my mom said. Something about castles. But she didn't mention Berlin." She'd paid so little attention to all the planning. Where they were going seemed irrelevant back then compared to the fact that they were leaving home at all.

"Bet it won't be as much fun as Bruges," Ben said, a crooked grin breaking out over his face.

They laughed.

"Definitely not." Birdie paused, not wanting to leave her new friends behind. "Well, I guess I should go. Get cleaned up."

Kayla opened her arms, and Birdie stepped into them. They hugged, and then Birdie turned to Ben.

"Stay out of trouble," she said.

"Never," he said. "Bye, Birdie."

She started down the hall toward the flight of stairs that

would lead her to the attic room for the last time.

"Hey, Birdie," he called after her.

"Yes?" She turned around to look at them.

"Do you still have the aventurine?"

She reached into her pocket. She'd completely forgotten about it in all the excitement. It was cool on her fingers as she pulled it out and held it for the others to see. They came closer to examine her outstretched hand.

The coppery glass was sparkling with golden flakes.

"The knight is gone," Ben said.

"So is the bear," Kayla said.

Birdie turned the aventurine over on her palm. Sparkles filled that side too.

She rubbed it, but nothing happened. The flakes didn't swirl, and the temperature didn't change.

"Great souvenir," Kayla said.

"Did you know that in French the word *souvenir* means 'memory'?" Ben asked.

Birdie slipped the aventurine into her pocket and smiled at Ben and Kayla.

"Then I will be sure to never forget you," she said. "Or this magical place."

ABOUT THE AUTHOR

Heidi Williamson loves to travel, study history, and write stories. When she's home, she's based in Pennsylvania. When she's not home, she spends time exploring beautiful places, both in the United States and abroad.

www.birdieabroad.com